THE DEVIL AND THE
DAIRY PRINCESS

BLUE LIGHT  BOOKS

INDIANA UNIVERSITY PRESS
INDIANA REVIEW

PEDRO PONCE

THE DEVIL

and the

DAIRY PRINCESS

Stories

BLUE LIGHT BOOKS

This book is a publication of

Indiana University Press
Office of Scholarly Publishing
Herman B Wells Library 350
1320 East 10th Street
Bloomington, Indiana 47405 USA

iupress.org

Manufactured in the United
States of America

Cataloging information is available
from the Library of Congress.

ISBN 978-0-253-05860-7 (paperback)
ISBN 978-0-253-05861-4 (ebook)

First Printing 2021

For My Parents

CONTENTS

ACKNOWLEDGMENTS

Much of this book was written at the Julia and David White Artists' Colony and the Banff Centre for Arts and Creativity. The author would like to acknowledge these residency programs as well as St. Lawrence University for their generous research support.

THE DEVIL AND THE
DAIRY PRINCESS

The Piazza de Chirico

Arcade

One does not enter so much as encounter the Piazza de Chirico. We
are roused by a strange conjunction of statuary and architecture: the
head of a horse emerging from an archway, a supine nymph fanned by
the spray of a fountain, the face of a clock emerging like a querulous
moon from behind the leaves of an artichoke. We avoid the arcade if
we have somewhere pressing to be. One moment, traffic harangues us
as we hazard a crowded crosswalk; the next, we turn onto a vacancy of
cobbles, lined by archways receding far into the distance. If we follow
our instincts—which, in the interests of propriety, we mostly ignore—
we pocket digital porters, ignore the ringtones of concerned friends or

fretful dates, and set off in the direction of diminishing columns. We are never alone in our fecklessness. Scattered like tribute at the base of pedestals are abandoned briefcases, purses, grocery bags, and bulging totes, which, never claimed, are discarded or collect dust on the shelves of the Lost & Found.

Kiosk

The piazza is not our most popular attraction. We are better known for our Rustic Quarter, which preserves the picturesque simplicity of another age, down to the elaborate glass fixtures that crown streetlamps. The Menagerie District is considered more family friendly, the Natural History Museum more edifying, the Botanical Preserve more picturesque, the Empyrean Falls more sublime. The piazza's proximity to the train station was intended to attract visitors with its convenient location. Despite the efforts of our Chamber of Commerce, attendance remains low. Brochures are careful to describe the park's distinct atmosphere as contemplative rather than desolate, its disorienting vistas a trick of design. Complaints nevertheless accumulate at the feedback kiosk, so many that piazza volunteers have been overwhelmed and replaced by boxes that, by the end of a given week, are packed with scrawled survey forms, their corners waving from crammed slots like flags raised in surrender.

Enigma

Regardless of how many times we wander the piazza, new vistas always reveal themselves. The Mannequin Grove lures us inward, limbs beckoning as if for partners in a dance. We traverse a series of deserted squares joined at corners that widen at our approach. The squares seem to rise acutely in our path, an optical illusion. Still, we are exhausted by the time we reach the furthest colonnade. The clock that marked our entrance is unreadable from this distance where we pause to catch our breath. In haste to retrace our steps, we almost miss the limbs of mannequins emerging from a nearby niche. They are posed exactly as they were where we began. Beyond the nearer brush, we hear the familiar chuff of delivery trucks, the cloying of chapel bells. We follow the noise to our point of origin, the same pavement traced by windblown refuse, the same awnings limp with rain.

Ariadne

Critics of the piazza are a small but vocal minority. Our election cycles invariably begin with weekly editorials calling for its redesign or demolition. Campaign buttons feature the iconic figure of Ariadne, who occupies the piazza's central square, her bare breasts obscured by a censor's opaque sash. Her profile is framed by slogans admonishing us to reclaim the moral fiber of our community. Despite this, no prevailing candidate has ever attempted to legislate the piazza's closure.

Ferry

Those who defend the piazza extol its cunning design: kaleidoscopic perspectives are created by the deft placement of stationary structures without the mechanical gimmickry employed by theme parks and other amusement franchises. Rumors persist, however, of hidden machinery, if not present from inception, then recently annexed in a desperate bid to swell flagging attendance. Silhouettes appear and vanish from windows and colonnades; shadows gather and extend with little conformity to the natural paths of sunlight; sails swell incongruously against the sides of tenements. We are dared to trace the trick to its source and end the mystery once and for all. We nod in determined complicity before discreetly changing the subject, unsure of what perturbs us more: the revelation of gears and levers or a waiting ferry poised on the shores of a nameless sea.

Voyage

We are a landlocked city. What we lack in venturesome terrain and romantic vistas, however, is offset by the values distilled from our native topography: integrity, moderation, forthrightness. We are consistently voted "Most Navigable" by the major travel magazines. Our streets map themselves in seamless grids on the memories of newcomers. Those seeking more variety may enjoy the man-made marvels of the Canal District or the natural wonders simulated twice daily at the Museum of Virtual Knowledge. We emerge to pristine food courts, our sleeves damp from rainforest dew or whitewater falls, the pavement at our feet rendered jagged by the scrim of stereo lenses. Eyes readjust to the unmediated taupe of bus shelters and city squares streaked in neon. We stutter homeward, blinking in the glare.

Tower

Brochures advertising the piazza make note of the eight towers that form an enchanting skyline within a skyline. This is an exaggeration, if not an outright fiction. There are at most two towers in the Piazza de Chirico: the Great Tower in the northwest corner and the Red Tower that bisects the southern wall. The others are merely versions of these two, seen from different angles further distinguished by the piazza's uncanny geometry. Some go even further, claiming that the two towers are one and the same, merely observed at different times of day. A growing faction agitates from the opposite view, claiming that there are indeed eight or perhaps more towers in the piazza and that praise for the imaginative design is a mere ruse to placate the taxpaying public.

Moon

In spring, the piazza extends its hours, opening to visitors after dark. Beneath the gloss of a full moon, sculpted fruit sprouts from the cobblestones with particular succulence. Even the passageways through desolate colonnades are not without their charm, threaded by silver moths and blossoming vines. Between a screening at the local art house and a late meal taken alfresco, couples often stroll the piazza's length, noting mutual reactions with dissembled interest. If nothing else, the moonlit vistas are fodder for conversation. The fortuitously paired will recognize a shared amusement at the strangeness of the piazza, indulging its wonders with the mild gasps and knowing laughter reserved for haunted houses or wax museums. A tree branch creaks overhead; footsteps echo from distant corners. We welcome the sudden clutch these provoke in our companions, the closeness afforded in traversing the unknown. We regain the well-lit avenues arm in arm. Yet occasionally, the piazza lingers beyond its role in our designs. We make small talk, consider menus, weave fingers emboldened by wine. Across the table, we sense an absence behind nods of understanding, a distraction focused just beyond.

Map

Despite repeated attempts by the Bureau of Public Works, no accurate map exists of the Piazza de Chirico. Every updated version is followed by weeks of indignant calls from parents led to dead ends on their way to birthday parties; breathless octogenarians lost to walking groups; weeping dog walkers who looked away for mere seconds; aspiring fiancés foiled at the crucial moment by the apparent disappearance of the Palm Grove. Indeed, the piazza is not one square but many. Its spaces proliferate with every visitor. From the height of the Great Tower, we could be looking at our kitchen tables, fruit ripening on a nearby sill, juice cooled in a fluted pitcher. From the ground, the pitcher acquires limbs and a torso; the speckled rind acquires the enormity of monumental sculpture. The overhanging loggia resembles a giant's backrest. Later, we will ignore amused whispers and irritated stares to finger transit tokens and cigarette lighters, toll slips and canned sardines, ruins newly excavated.

Shadow

There are days we resent the piazza. Its stark vacancies strike us as bland, its poetic appositions cloying and crude. We forsake its shadowy cloisters for the aisles of the All-Mart. We relish the store's tidy geometry, shelves piled with all manner of tangible distractions: bowling balls, fishing rods, tires, plastic lawn fixtures, oven cleaner, stock pots, dish cubbies, doorstops, espadrilles, hiking cleats, aromatic candles, concealers, revealers, duvets, bathing salts, cosmetic masks, analgesics. We fill baskets, carts, and canvas bags. We sign for the total, names etched in duplicate. Traffic swells at our return; we signal by horn and gesture the urgency that impels us. Amid construction cones and terraces of blinking letters, the piazza's turnstiles sway feebly in the rusting light.

Clock

Visitors are surrounded by clocks, mounted on pediments overhead and reputedly accurate. There is thus no excuse for malingering. Nevertheless, we find ourselves giving the same excuse to skeptical faces: we lost track of time. How to explain the experience of the piazza, where time is marked not by what is happening but what is about to happen? The houselights dim. A curtain rises. We wait, silenced before the bare stage.

Still Life

The story is told of a voluble matron—never a native of these parts—who accompanied her more saturnine husband to the piazza for an afternoon. Her amazed exclamations funneled bluntly from between faraway columns, coaxing birds from the porticos. She resolved to record every monument and trick of perspective for the benefit of her book club back home, eagerly notifying each recipient using the phone function on her camera. So distracted was she by her growing collection—the Great Tower a mere trinket pinched between fingers, a display of mock terror at the giant fish on stilts—that she was soon separated from her husband. She ignored his absence until sudden hunger reminded her that she had skipped lunch in an effort to stay on itinerary. She searched with growing concern, spotting him at last in a narrow corridor formed by the back legs of a rearing horse in bronze. She would later recall how she recognized him in minute detail, despite the intervening distance—his scalp, burnished to a dull rose by an excess of sun cream, his shirt collar dog-eared to one side despite her patient smoothing on the shuttle downtown. He faced away, in the direction of an empty expanse walled in by segments of brick and freestanding columns; she could discern him raising his camera—as always, reluctantly, for he could never be bothered to document the most picturesque parts of their trips. She forgot her annoyance, relieved at the prospect of departing for an early supper. She was only vaguely aware in her eagerness of how the scene eluded any apparent progress, how the surrounding buildings seemed to rank ever more tightly at either side of a diminishing aspect. Conscious of the time, she quickened her

The Devil and the Dairy Princess

steps. The blow came directly to the face, her just lowered wristwatch eliminating any chance of dulling the impact. She never lost consciousness—an important factor forestalling litigation. At her feet, an easel creaked to rest. The sky of her vision, tufted with clouds, the brick and stone baked to gold in the afternoon sun, bore the dimple of her forehead. A corner of the toppled canvas drew her eyes toward a darkening plinth.

Fountain

On a typical visit, we pause before one of the piazza's fountains, stark quadrangular basins centered on a single narrow spout. We dig in our pockets for spare change, indulging the traveler's custom of tossing coins to the trickling waters to earn a speedy return. We find our tokens but hesitate over the burbling stone, wondering what's the use. We know we will return, whether from nearby stoops and offices or from distant chambers steeped in the rarest dust.

Melancholy

Those who favor the piazza's closure see it as more than a drain on public resources. Anecdotal evidence—given greater credence by the occasional exposé on the evening news—suggests that visitors experience a range of symptoms associated with their wanderings, mostly short-term melancholy but also occasional anxiety, intermittent panic, and suicidal thoughts. We are discouraged from returning by concerned community leaders, who encourage more salutary distractions in newspaper editorials and posted bills. For a time, we resume long-abandoned hobbies, tackle living quarters with sprays and dusters, browse catalogs of interior design. At odd moments, we muse on the disarray of our industry, skeins of wool and spilled flour, chicken wire and wallpaper, motor oil and calisthenic balls, compost and muffin tins—tableaux familiar from dreams, purged of alchemy.

Glove

The piazza subsists on donations, the occasional hosting fee for large events, and sales of merchandise. Postcards sell briskly, as do bookends pairing miniatures of the piazza's best-known landmarks: the Red

Tower, the Endless Arcade, the marble bust of Apollo. Less popular are the pastries and biscuits modeled on the outsize specimens festooning monoliths scattered throughout the grounds—stale and chalky, these often melt to unappetizing mush at the base of our morning coffee. For a time, a version of the enormous hand pointing the way to Lovers Grove was a popular souvenir. It remains a striking fixture of the odd costume party, sporting event, or price-slashing storefront.

Train

We have a train to catch. There is always a train to catch, but this train, the train we await on this platform, cannot be missed. We have arrived even earlier than usual to ensure catching it with time to spare. The newspapers, customarily perused as we wait, remain folded beneath our coat sleeves. Perhaps the corner of a page ripples to distract us, but we ignore it, fixing our sights firmly on the vacant track. We check our watches; the dials are blurred by mist. We wipe fastidiously at the slick glass. In the distance, a keening engine approaches. We move quickly to join the growing rank bordering the platform's edge. Legs bar our progress, splayed rigidly over briefcases and blood-colored loafers. The louder the engine's approach, the deeper the thicket of legs, arched ever higher against the horizon. We see smoke funnel sluggishly into the pale sky, a line of cars dark as beetle backs, the cuff of the attendant, our palms spread empty before the jaws of his ticket punch. We start to sprint, our progress arrested by plush carpet, furrowed pillows, and the questioning faces of cats.

Interior

We never wander the piazza aimlessly. We always have a destination, however veiled by the derangement that pauses our steps. We seek the interior, the origin of the piazza's divergent footpaths. If attained, some believe, the significance of its design will be apprehended in full, revealing the secret architecture of all space. Others dismiss this as, at best, amusing folklore for tourists, and at worst, yet another symptom of our compulsion for symmetry.

The Devil and the Dairy Princess

Corridor

We sink into repose under shady archways, lulled by the chime of fountains. But we startle just at the point of giving over, our fingers making pale fists at our sides. We shake off stupor and rise to the exits. We conduct the day's remaining business with particular diligence and expediency. A satisfying exhaustion loosens our necks and shoulders as we make our way home. In the after-hours din, we gossip over pints and tumblers, cheering another day's end. At some point, caught between conversations, we opt for neither and instead search the street outside. Moonlight traces the dim outlines of lowered grates, mute hydrants, the bobbing heads of sleeping men casting for dreams.

Curtain

To those who avoid the piazza and those who habitually wander its paths, one may add a third group. At one time, they, too, were habitual wanderers, by far the most frequent. Once acquainted with the piazza's expanse, they would spend entire days there, convinced of eventually mastering its secret. Their search would lead them to obscure corners rarely frequented by the public—an archway's looming vacancy, the curtained void between ornamental statues. They vacillated before the hieroglyph of monument and minutiae. They watched the curtain ripple over stone seams, revealing a wedge of shadow. Walls made firm by trick of light opened out into thresholds scattered with sand. Their hesitancy overcome, they turned in the direction of their entry, never to return.

The Discovery of
Dr. James Osborne Beckett

James Osborne Beckett stared nervously at the napkin in his lap. His companion, whom he had known in college as Lauren Bryce but who was now Lauren Miller in the eyes of God and the Commonwealth of Massachusetts, drank eagerly from her water glass, tilting ice into her mouth and relishing its freshness. She had been on her feet all day; exhaustion and thirst caused her to forget her usually delicate manners. She spoke around the dwindling sliver, peppering Beckett with spray as she quizzed him on the progress of his postdoctorate in the Magnetic Fields Laboratory of Anselmo Polytechnic.

Beckett demurred, crumbling a stick of bread to powder on his plate. Miller smiled in mock offense. "You know I'm pretty smart for a civilian," she said, using Beckett's term of disparagement for the non-scientist. She had managed to survive introductory chemistry, with significant help from Beckett, before leaving science altogether to double major in French and art history. Now a museum curator, she had made the five-hour trip west of her home in the Berkshires to attend Anselmo's annual Representational Technologies Conference and catch up with her close friend of ten years.

Beckett looked at Miller, his expression unchanged. "What's wrong?" Miller asked.

"Too much time in the lab, I guess." Beckett leaned back in his seat.

The doctor had, in fact, diagnosed himself correctly. He had spent too many hours toiling without result in his studies of electromagnetism. His failures at work had prompted him to contemplate his other, more personal failures, the most glaring of which was failing to confess his love of Lauren Bryce, now Miller, which had begun from the moment he had first seen her shuffling awkwardly to reggae beneath the maples of their alma mater. He was not foolish enough to save himself for the hoped-for day when she would look at him with something more than the affection inspired by sexual irrelevance. He was, however, foolish enough to imbue their decade of drunken confidences and happenstance proximity—at this juncture, a matter of a single state line—with the design of fate. After yet another unproductive week, he had been surprised by her voice on his answering machine, asking if he could join her for lunch. In the intervening days, he had decided that he would at last break his silence. There was, of course, no chance of fulfillment; as he took a sip of water, the diamond on Miller's finger winked an ominous semaphore. But if his life's work were to amount to nothing, at the very least he would have a definitive answer for the one question that now seemed the only one worth asking.

Miller, for her part, had always suspected something. In college, when his feelings were all but spelled out in the detritus of a Saturday night, she would tell herself she was flattered and coax him toward the nearest water fountain. She would even consider yielding to his desire once better prospects had fallen through. (They had kissed once, at a party celebrating a rare win in football during the fall of their sophomore year; neither would remember on waking the following afternoon.) Now, as Beckett struggled to put his feelings into words, Miller reminded herself that this was not a chance encounter with a cavalier stranger. This was Jamie Beckett, who had seen her through the divorce of her parents, the death of a grandmother, and countless rejections, personal and professional. As awkward as it would be, she had to treat her friend with the sensitivity he deserved.

"You fucking idiot." Diners at surrounding tables swiveled slightly in their seats, glancing askance. "Did you . . . what did you . . . what do you expect me to say?"

"I don't expect anything."

"Bullshit," she said. "If you didn't expect anything, you wouldn't have brought it up."

Beckett ran his hands through his hair and folded them behind his head. "This was a mistake."

"You think?"

"I thought . . . I thought I could tell you without it getting weird."

"Oh, give me a fucking break," Miller said. She bit savagely into a warm roll. "There's always a line, a limit. Do you think I was always honest with you?"

"Weren't you?"

Miller shook her head and swallowed.

"What about Mr. Software Developer? You always honest with him?"

"That's different," she said.

"Is it really so terrible? The idea of you and me—"

"Of course it is. What? You think looser pants makes them easier to get into?"

By now, Beckett had noticed the stares from other tables. "OK, I get it," he said.

"I don't think you do. This changes everything."

"It doesn't have to."

"Oh, right. Because this is just one of those bumps in the road, right? We'll look back on this someday and laugh? In case you haven't noticed, my someday is booked pretty solid for the foreseeable future. I don't need this right now."

"Sorry," Beckett replied. "Guess I should be grateful for the hour you managed to spare."

"And what the fuck is that—" She squeezed her eyes shut. "Sorry," she said.

"That's OK. I probably deserve it."

"I wasn't talking to you." Miller lowered her hands to the rise of her maternity blouse. "She hears things."

"It's a girl?"

Miller smiled and nodded.

Beckett stared at the taut silk, halved by a placket of pearl buttons. It was at this moment that the scientist could see, as if projected on a spherical screen, the topography of Earth's magnetic field emerge with preternatural clarity across the expanse of Miller's belly. The murmur of conversation and clanking at adjacent tables, the halting apologies which were now indeed meant for him from Lauren's side of their corner booth—after this, Beckett and Miller would never see each other again—all receded as Beckett tracked the movement of waves from pole to pole. He then came to two conclusions as Miller waited for him to speak: First, if magnetism traveled the planet's surface along predictable lines of force, much like the pattern formed by metal filings held over a small magnet, then these lines could be warped and their energy harnessed to expedite the traffic of any number of objects over long distances. Second, if there was anything of destiny inherent to his relation to Miller, he was now witnessing its fruition and extent. Wordlessly, Beckett rose from his seat, leaving Miller to pay the tab.

Francesca Reed Miller was born at 11:10 in the morning on November 22, 1999, at Greylock Regional Hospital near Briggsville, Massachusetts. Two days overdue, she weighed in at eight pounds, eleven ounces.

Whether Beckett's revelation yielded any results is a matter beyond the public record. A survey of relevant scientific journals yields no articles carrying his byline; he vanishes from newspaper and magazine accounts after the announcement of his postdoctoral research award in the spring of 1998. By the conclusion of his three-year fellowship, one can surmise either that his research was considered too speculative to merit support by his otherwise preoccupied homeland, or it was too valuable to continue development beyond government scrutiny. One fact is indisputable: citing economic strictures and a swelling student body, Anselmo Polytechnic closed operation of its Magnetic Fields Laboratory in December 2001, announcing plans to use the site for new student housing. To this day, the site remains empty.

Neighbors within a one-mile radius of the lab had always blamed its proximity for regular disruptions of electrical and other services to their living units. The laboratory's closure did little to abate panicked calls to service providers and emergency personnel at all hours with reports of dead phone lines, frozen wireless access, and strange fires localized around toasters, space heaters, and other appliances operating via electrically charged coils.

For Maria Purpurin, an assistant at Anselmo's central library, the closure coincided with phenomena stranger still. Having survived a difficult day toward the end of Anselmo's winter break, all she wanted was a hot bath, complemented by a glass of Shiraz, her one indulgence in a life of otherwise monastic restraint. Her glass, filled nearly to the top, splashed wine at her feet as she reached blindly for the bathroom light. She took two irritated gulps as she punched the switch. She set her glass down and began undoing her robe when she noticed her boyfriend, Jeremy Tyndall, standing fully dressed in the tub. This by itself was not unusual; the couple had decided to spend the New Year's weekend together before both resumed their respective unaccommodating schedules. What led Purpurin, in her astonishment, to mistake Tyndall for an intruder and hurl the wineglass at his face was the fact that, just that morning, she had dropped him off at the local airport, from where he was to catch the next shuttle and resume his duties as an associate for an intellectual property boutique in Chicago.

Tyndall caught the glass in his right hand, but not before it bounced painfully off the bridge of his nose and burned his eyes with its contents.

"Honeysuckle," said the wounded patents lawyer, squinting blindly in Purpurin's direction, "what the fuck?"

At the sound of her nickname, a shibboleth preserved only for their most intimate moments, Purpurin collapsed to the floor. The last

The Devil and the Dairy Princess

thing she saw before closing her eyes was Tyndall stooping to catch her before his hands seemed to turn transparent against the tiles overhead.

When Purpurin opened her eyes, she could discern the corner of the sink and the very tip of the roseate light fixture. She smelled spilled wine and was quickly convinced that the events preceding her fall were mere visions stoked by exhaustion and inebriation. The year before, when she had first met Tyndall, then a third-year student at Anselmo's Llewellyn Chambers School of Law, she knew his ambition would carry him far, but she was not prepared for the actual distance separating Briggsville Regional and O'Hare. Daily phone dates dwindled to semimonthly exchanges between errands and the exigencies of their respective careers. The prospect of an actual visit was deferred to the week before Halloween, then the week of Thanksgiving, before being postponed to the New Year. Their long weekend together felt shortened from the start by the imminence of departure, though they made the most of it, huddled in bed against Purpurin's faulty heating as Dick Clark welcomed the year 2002. They had both resolved to see more of each other in the coming year, and she had survived Tyndall's vanishing through the security gate without a single tear. But as she made her way to the parking level exit, she passed a pair of armed guards, who at this point were still patrolling Briggsville at regular intervals. She dropped her purse in front of a vacant baggage carousel and stood sobbing for several minutes, until the attention of one of the guards prompted her to leave. When she told the story later, she ascribed her sadness to citizenship in a restive country sprung up seemingly overnight. What she never mentioned was how the patrol, their guns wielded at acute angles, imbued Tyndall's departure with a permanence she had struggled all that weekend to ignore.

And yet, here he was, lingering even in Purpurin's presumed sobriety. He leaned over delicately, propped on the rim of the tub by his rumpled pin-striped sleeves.

"I've figured it out," he said. "As long as I stay in the tub, this . . . whatever it is holds up."

Carefully, as if testing the temperature, Purpurin lowered a bare foot, nestling it between the cuffs of Tyndall's trousers. She braced for him at any moment to vanish again, but his substance held, squeezing reassuringly around her ankle. She felt sure enough with her next step to run her other foot playfully along his calf as, using the fixtures at her waist for support, she turned herself around and nestled slowly into the crook formed by Tyndall's body. She ignored the pain in her right shoulder as it ground against the tub's rim, the smears of lint from his moistened socks, and lapped eagerly at the musky underside of his chin.

It is not necessary to elaborate further on the couple's discovery; it is sufficient to say that for the first two months of their circumscribed intimacy, they existed together in a curious limbo of excess and deprivation. The novelty of their union inspired unprecedented creativity in both as together, they catalogued in the soreness of undiscovered muscles every possibility imaginable in showerhead, towel bar, elastic hose, and diverter valve. They marked their favorite positions with textured adhesives shaped like daisies, hibiscus flowers, and tropical fish that scratched bracingly at their spent limbs while they gossiped about their respective days. Tyndall's nemesis at the firm was a name partner who compensated for his erectile dysfunction by inducing panic attacks in underlings. Purpurin, whose significant attractions were further augmented by the librarian's spectacles and professional dress, was daily subject to the most inept flirtations by fellow clerks, graduate students, and even a balding assistant professor who, claiming complete ignorance of the library's computer search system, rewarded her patient explanations with capsule histories of the most salient technical innovations of ancient Greece and Rome, ostensibly closer to his bailiwick.

Tyndall growled jealously into Purpurin's ear. "What's his name?" he asked, making a fist.

Purpurin brushed her fingers softly over the side of his belly, where he was especially ticklish. "You're a goose," she said, sliding her arm firmly around him.

There were, however, rules and limitations. Tyndall could occupy both his own space and the liminal space of the tub some thousand miles away. But Purpurin could, at best, thrust her arm up to the elbow into Chicago before she was repulsed with a force that, more than once, knocked her flush to the shower wall. And more than once, their lovemaking was interrupted when, in the process of minor adjustment

The Devil and the Dairy Princess

augmented by an inopportune clutch, Tyndall was tripped into premature withdrawal through the portal, the dimensions of which were eventually established, through trial and error, as roughly three feet by four feet to the lower right of the showerhead.

The most significant limitation was the least apparent. Within their improvised bower, Purpurin and Tyndall made up a world every bit as vivid and expansive as the one they shed at the edges of Dr. Beckett's contingency. But beyond, their interludes together took on the savor of dreams vaguely remembered on waking. Girlfriends offered Purpurin any number of possibilities culled from the area's most sensitive and enterprising bachelors; she refused all with uncharacteristic vehemence. Tyndall's colleagues were less systematic as they coaxed their friend from lap dance to lap dance, grimly endured until his next otherworldly assignation.

At this point, a larger question arises: Why not confide to others the miracle of Beckett's research? We are left to speculate: either they were willing subjects of experimentation, trading silence for sufficient funds to support their eventual reunion on a more stable plane, or they alone conspired to hide their odd conjunction, the better at first to hoard its sweetness for themselves and, subsequently, to deny the fragility exposed in preserving it. In time, she came to relish those evenings when she could enjoy the luxurious vacancy of her apartment while he diligently billed hours. He knew that one day, he would ignore altogether the beckoning hand between wallpaper stripes urging him on in the labor of bliss.

Maria Purpurin was married on June 19, 2003, at Bradley Pavilion in Briggsville. The groom, a professor of technological history and culture at Anselmo Polytechnic, plastered flat the strands of his combover in a manner that, he was assured, was adorable before taking his bride for their inaugural spin, set to Sinatra's "It Had to Be You."

The Presentation

He had been warned about the City, its size, its seductions. He had lived all his life in the City's shadow, walking to school against its distant skyline, imagining a life there once he had grown older. But he had never left his native town.

Now he was being summoned there for business. He nodded to his superior and retreated to his cubicle, barely acknowledging the curious looks that followed him. He was a competent worker who had already been promoted once; that he was being entrusted with business in the City was a sure sign that he had a long future ahead with the Company. He set these thoughts aside as he made the necessary arrangements.

* * *

The City, at first sight, was disappointing. As the Central Terminal stop was announced, he watched a slowing procession of squat, drab buildings intermittently marked by stenciled numbers and graffiti. Darkness enveloped the car; passengers blinked sluggishly under the chalky lights overhead. He emerged into a narrow corridor of bodies, all vying for passage up the same escalator.

At street level, the air felt suddenly cooler. He flinched at the sudden frigidity of his neck, damp from his efforts to simultaneously guard his luggage, find the appropriate exit gate, and look for the liaison who was to meet him at the terminal.

"Need ride?" he heard a voice call behind him.

He turned to see a sallow-faced man reaching for one of his bags. "I'm waiting for someone," he replied as forcefully as he could, pulling the bag away. He was still out of breath from the rush up the escalator.

The stranger was insistent. "No problem. I take. I take." He reached again for one of the bags.

From the periphery of his growing panic, he heard a woman's voice. "Is there a problem?" she said. She positioned herself between them. "I'll take it from here, thank you." On the clipboard she grasped at her waist, he saw his name printed neatly in black ink. He followed her out the sliding glass doors of the exit corridor.

As he slid next to her into the company car, he struggled to remember her name. At a retreat last year, he had learned the power of names and how using them immediately on learning them would help you to remember them, creating greater intimacy with prospective clients. He had forgotten to do this just now in his relief at leaving the terminal.

"Thanks for helping me out back there . . . Claire." He dragged the name out under his breath in case it might have been Clara.

Her smile in response had a practiced warmth that was impossible to read. "No problem," she said. "It's not nearly as bad as when I moved here."

"From where?"

"The West Coast."

Within two blocks, traffic was already thick. Their conversation was frequently interrupted by the driver's acceleration into the nearest open lane. They stopped midway through the Septage District. As they waited for the traffic lights to change, a crew of workers in dark jumpsuits probed a tangle of tubes springing up through a hole in the sidewalk. One of the workers pulled at the thickest tube with a free hand; it slipped from his grasp and slid to the pavement, attached by thin strands of slime to the worker's glove. The worker coaxed the tubing back to the crook of his arm and withdrew a square black case from his back pocket. In one fluid motion, a blade emerged from the case and fixed itself to the pale surface of the tube. The worker's grasp tightened as he made several short incisions. The tube looked hard on the outside, but when the worker peeled back the area he had cut, he exposed a rosy interior swollen with soft reticulations. The car began to fill with a dank, fecal smell.

"How long have you worked for the Company?" he asked.

"Three years. What about you?"

"This is my sixth."

"Wow. Six years. How do you like it?"

The lights changed. The car accelerated, clipping his answer to a distracted mumble. He raised his voice to make sure he was understood. "Great. Really great."

She looked at him for a moment and nodded. "I don't see myself staying much longer."

"Really?"

Her smile turned coy. She pressed a finger to her lips. Candor brought a pleasant tilt to her otherwise plain features.

"What will you do instead?"

"I don't know. I model part time."

"You do?"

"Are you surprised?"

"No. Of course not. I guess . . . I never expected to meet a real model my first time to the City."

"There are more of us than you'd think," she said. She sounded slightly defensive as she perused the clipboard on her lap.

They stopped again, this time right before a traffic circle bordering Downtown. At either side of their turgid lane, scaffolding and terraces of chain-link fence rose in ragged walls, flagged with the names of construction companies and banners advertising rental rates.

"So much construction," he said. "When'll it all be finished?"

"Most of these are mock-ups." She smiled at his confused expression. "The City claims a number of blocks annually for staging demolition and construction. The mayor calls it 'Progressive Ideation.' Something about being able to see signs of progress from every block in every borough. It's actually a very cost-effective program. Most of the employees are out-of-work actors. My boyfriend played a welder for three months at a site on Seventh Avenue. They gave him a hard hat, face shield, a torch that shot real sparks—even one of those black lunch pails that opens in half."

"Does he still work for the City?"

"I wouldn't know. Once he could make rent, he lost interest in sharing a place."

"Sorry."

"I'm not. He looked good in those overalls. But he was never any good with his hands."

His hotel appeared beyond the tinted glass. Its windows stretched the length of the entire block.

"I have a show tomorrow night." The liaison dug through a pocket of her bag and handed him a black-and-white flyer. It resembled an old-fashioned movie poster. A woman clutched both sides of her face midscream, her mouth forming a dark ellipse. Above her was written in grotesquely dripping letters: CRIMES OF FASHION. "You should come. Just tell them I sent you."

"I will. Definitely." He thanked the liaison as he got out, folding the flyer and putting it in one of his overcoat pockets. He watched the company car vanish into the late afternoon traffic until he was startled by the burgundy sleeve of the bellman asking for his bag.

* * *

He decided to stay in, ordering room service and going over his presentation one more time. He was in bed by 10:30 p.m., hoping to get to the office by 7:45 a.m. after a quick shower and breakfast. He tossed restlessly for half an hour before resigning himself to sleeplessness and whatever was on television.

He paused at a wide shot of his hotel. He thought he recognized the same bellman who had taken his bags after the liaison dropped him off.

An attractive woman in a burgundy skirt and blazer said "Welcome" in English, and her words were translated into other languages at the top and bottom of the screen. She went on to wish the viewer a safe and happy stay, urging caution in stowing one's valuables and opening one's door to strangers. He began to nod off as the woman explained the icons for laundry, room service, and other amenities accessible through the in-room phone. In profile, a hotel guest could be seen sleeping soundly to the reassuring voice of the woman in burgundy. He adjusted his pillow in order to see the screen more clearly. The woman's voice grew louder; he could feel it bristling through his skull. He sat up. The television was off. He watched himself breathing in the dimness of the screen.

* * *

He arrived right at 8:00 a.m. and was welcomed by the liaison from the previous day. She led him to a large conference room that looked out on the City's northern skyline. Two enormous cranes bobbed and swayed against the overcast gray. He wondered if these were real work crews or the imitations described yesterday on the ride from the terminal. He followed two of the workers, tiny figures at street level, as they consulted unscrolled diagrams with gestures of interest that seemed vaguely exaggerated. He felt a tap on his shoulder, and his nose nearly brushed a pale hand offered stiffly in greeting.

The hand belonged to a wiry man in a striped charcoal suit. His face was smooth, but his hair was thin, plastered in an ornate garland to his skull. "Sorry about that," the man said, indicating one of the chairs facing away from the window. "I was in Processing for several years before my last promotion. Bad for the eyes. First time in the City?"

"Yes," he replied, unzipping his briefcase and removing his notes and projector. "Very impressive."

The Devil and the Dairy Princess

"I'm glad," the man said, as he took one of the seats opposite. He folded his hands together, propping his chin on pressed fingers. The stripes on his lapel indicated management level. "The City can be quite overwhelming one's first time through."

"Oh, it certainly is. But . . . in a good way."

The Manager grinned. "Yes. Well, at any rate, welcome. We are very eager to hear your report."

He nodded and displayed the first slide. His recall, by this point, was automatic, and he had to make sure to take his time so that his tone did not turn rote. The first slide, a graph representing the last decade of quarterly expenditures, required him to approach in order to indicate a relevant two-year segment. From his suit coat pocket, he took out the collapsible pointer he had special ordered through the office supplier in town. He approached the screen, listening to the clicks as he opened the pointer. The clicks were muted by his voice reciting percentages and invoice numbers and the percussion of a jackhammer outside. He returned intermittently to the conference table to consult his notes. The glossy mahogany seemed to pen him further into the vista of traffic and scaffolding at his back. The glare of the track lights intensified, until his audience all but vanished into the walls behind it.

The Manager and liaison were applauding. "Well done," said the Manager. "Don't you think?" The liaison jotted something down on her tablet screen without looking up.

The Manager excused himself. Before he left, he handed over a small manila envelope. "You've earned yourself a night off. On us. Enjoy." He fished briefly with both hands for a firm congratulatory shake.

The liaison stayed behind as he packed up his things. "I wouldn't worry about it," she said. "Everyone's a bit nervous presenting the first time."

He looked at her. "I thought it went pretty well."

"Of course," said the liaison. She took a sip from a steaming mug.

When he reached the lobby, he checked his watch. It was 9:13 a.m. The sun had appeared and was blanching the storefronts outside. In town, he had been given numerous suggestions for how to spend his day in the City. The main office was only two blocks from Museum

Row and three subway stops from Central Park. He squeezed into the narrowing berth of a revolving door and emerged into a blinding wind that cut through his clothes. He followed the map provided earlier by the concierge back to his hotel.

* * *

He awoke at five in the afternoon to the digital chirp of his room phone. For several moments, he wondered if he had yet to begin his day. The seam between his drawn curtains was the orange of early morning; his mouth had the coppery savor of long, uninterrupted sleep. He fumbled the receiver to his ear.

"Hello?" he asked.

"Will you be needing the services of our cleaning staff today?"

"No," he answered. The automated message continued with more options. When he had pressed the number for no service, the voice wished him a good evening.

The Manager's envelope contained a sheaf of restaurant recommendations, an expense card, and a ticket to something called *The Presentation*. Several of the restaurant flyers featured ads describing it as "the theater experience of the season." A picture showed the small cast midperformance, one actor pointing in accusation, another looking aside, in the direction of the audience.

He had enough time before the show to walk toward the Theater District and find somewhere to eat. The farther he followed the side streets, the more redolent the air became with spice and smoked meat. Lines of people emerged from every doorway and corner stand. He watched maître d's wrangling impatient diners to their tables, waiters navigating narrow aisles behind stacked chafing dishes, baristas frothing milk and pouring foam into tiny ceramic bowls. He passed baskets heaped with dried frogs and feathered bodies dripping from hooks. He had eaten nothing since breakfast, but the more choices he encountered, the less hungry he was. He stopped at a traffic light blinking red over a line of puddles. Only half the signal seemed to work; the other half showed dark in the intermittent light, a bruise of crushed metal. The signal turned. He was jostled aside by a rush to the crosswalk. He kept his place on the pavement and stared at the inscrutable awnings that receded toward a distant boulevard. The nearest street sign was a rusty palimpsest.

He checked his watch. Only ten minutes remained until the start of the show. Midway down the next block, he recognized the darkened edges of a marquee. The ticket booth was lit. He approached the ticket taker inside for directions. The ticket taker regarded him blankly. A small window slid open, and the ticket taker asked to see his pass. He took the ticket and studied it closely before tearing it along the perforation and returning the stub. He announced a section and seat number before returning his attention to a pile of unsorted change.

The play, for the most part, consisted of obscenities repeated in various cadences. The obscenities were polysyllabic at comedic points in the narrative and monosyllabic when the story took a more serious turn. The central characters were a man and a woman who shared a mysterious past. The man had come back to reclaim something, something the woman kept in a rectangular tin she would open and contemplate during each of her soliloquies. Near the close of the first act, the man interrupted a bitter exchange with a request to use the woman's bathroom. "Isn't that how it always is," the woman said as the man stormed into the wings, "retreating to tend that sad, swollen sac. Fuck," she said softly, reaching for her tin.

He shifted in his seat, stifling a yawn. He felt the fullness of his own bladder. He navigated the dark between sections and left the auditorium. Squinting at the lobby's sudden light, he stumbled in the direction of the lavatories. The men's room was narrow and overheated, and beneath the sting of antibacterial soap, he smelled the sulfurous air from yesterday's car ride.

At the dappled marble sink, he recognized the actor who had just left the stage. He had laid aside his fedora and was smoothing the unruly strands of his comb-over.

"Great work," he said as the actor ran his hands under the soap dispenser. The actor paused briefly in his ministrations but resumed without even a glance into the speckled mirror. Replacing his fedora, he buttoned his coat and left the lavatory.

He followed shortly after and was about to open the auditorium door when he was stopped by one of the ushers, who pointed to the placard over the central pair of doors:

FOR THE ENJOYMENT OF OTHERS
AND OUR FINE ENSEMBLE
PATRONS NOT READMITTED
UNTIL NEXT INTERMISSION

"But—" he began. The usher silenced him with a raised hand. He had no idea how much longer this act would go on. He started to ask for a program but was again silenced. He folded his arms and heard a crinkling in his coat pocket. The liaison's flyer. Behind him, the auditorium erupted in laughter. He found the address and left to hail a cab.

* * *

He sat through a procession of gaunt figures displaying clothes cut from the same palette of pearl, charcoal, scarlet, and mist. The models entered from beneath an enormous banner on which the word EVASION appeared in enormous, fading type. Small cameras were mounted along the walkway at various levels, projecting images on three screens simultaneously. The images had the stark, grainy look of surveillance footage; the date and time appeared at the bottom of each screen. The clothes took on striking textures flattened onto the screens overhead. Heels shone with reptilian sleekness. Shot at torso level, a pencil skirt was cut just high enough to flash the seam of a stocking at every step. The model in the pencil skirt looked like the liaison but lacked her modest figure when she removed her jacket, beneath which bulged a mist-colored blouse.

He found the liaison framed by Camera 2, her face pressed to the runway between forked heels. Her eyes and mouth were open; a dark streak dribbled from her lips. He looked down from the screen and found her among the bodies outlined in chalk marking the models' path. Despite the loud pulse of percussion and the occasional stab of stilettos inches from her face, she maintained her death mask, never blinking during those intervals when her face was visible onscreen.

He was surprised when she found him after the show. She had yet to change out of her stage clothes. The fake blood on her face had dried into an asymmetrical crust. "Can you do me a favor?" she asked. She handed him a wallet camera. "I wanted some pictures before I get completely out of character. The trades all say corpses are going to be big this year." She led him into a changing room where blank walls bristled with pins.

She lay flat at his feet. Her blouse rose to reveal the smoothness of her belly.

"Are you trying to look down my pants?"

"No," he responded, moving the viewfinder.

She laughed, her cheeks vivid against the bare floor. "Stop," she said.

"What?"

"You're making me—" She squinted as she laughed harder, turning on her side and huffing into the crook of her arm. "OK," she announced before resuming her prone position. She stared at the pins overhead. She tensed for a moment, then went completely limp. Her blush vanished. Her skin seemed to absorb the gray hue of the dressing room floor. He aimed and shot.

There was a knock at the door. The doorway was blocked by a tall figure who looked dressed for the runway.

"We still going out?" It was a woman's voice.

"Yeah," the liaison said. She stood up. "This is—" He nodded at the garble made of his name.

The model looked him up and down without introducing herself. "We better hurry before curfew."

"Curfew?" he asked. "I thought that wasn't until . . ." He looked at his watch. "Shit . . ."

"You should come with us," the liaison said. "It's your last night."

Her friend was pushing buttons on her Toggle, her lips resembling the wax imitations he would get at carnivals as a child. The model's lips were silver. They barely flinched as he agreed to join them.

*   *   *

They were still blocks from their destination when the liaison's friend slowed her steps and began to dig through her purse. Despite the cold, her legs were bare. She wasn't shivering, but she stamped her pumps impatiently as she searched.

"Here we go," she said. She withdrew her fist and gestured with it to the liaison. The liaison bounced excitedly as she accepted one white capsule and a small plastic cup. "A little after-work pick-me-up," her friend added. "The guy I know has to order weeks in advance." She said this vaguely in his direction.

The liaison popped the capsule without a word to either of them. Her eyes and mouth closed with a satisfied expression before she resumed walking. She kept the cup palmed in her right hand.

They crossed an avenue and continued east. The liaison's friend monitored their progress on her Toggle, stopping to take the occasional call. Her answers to whoever called were terse and reluctant. "No," she said. "We're on our way. . . . We got held up."

The liaison had begun to shuffle rhythmically under the orange streetlights. They turned a corner and in the distance, he could hear the pulse of music, its rhythm matching the liaison's perfectly. At a stalled crosswalk, she leaned into him, facing the street. She pulled his arms around her and swayed against him. He leaned into her and felt the coldness of her earlobe against his mouth.

The light changed and the liaison bounded to the next corner. When he reached the other side, he saw she was staring into her empty cup. Her jaws worked quickly at the air, tasting it in shortening breaths. Her mouth closed abruptly and then opened in a long yawn. Her neck muscles contorted as she bent delicately over the cup and expelled a thin stream of orange fluid. Her friend's spasms were more intense, her clutch at the cup causing thin white cracks to form in the plastic. Orange beads formed along the sides as she filled the cup with her retching. She gulped the frothy contents before they could spill to the street. She sopped with her tongue at drops that stained her fingers. Their eyes met as she worked her thumb slowly out of her mouth.

He looked away, into a brightness at the edge of his vision. They had arrived. A long line snaked around the corner opposite. At the visible end, people waited for entrance into a rosy corridor surmounted by

The Devil and the Dairy Princess

letters that filled and refilled with liquid light: DREAMHOUSE. The liaison's friend went to talk to the bouncer at the front of the line. The liaison resumed dancing in place. The music inside was drowned out by a police patrol broadcasting the chimes for one hour to curfew. On the sides of the black van, a narrow screen displayed the current threat level. The liaison danced defiantly into the passing din; several booed or hoisted middle fingers. He turned to find the bouncer gesturing to him impatiently, the velvet barrier inches from being reclasped. He ran through the gap, mumbling his thanks.

He recognized no one in the security line. He was further delayed by the removal of his coat, belt, and shoes. He emerged alone into a slightly larger room. The color of the walls changed at regular intervals from deep red to deep blue. The source was a miniature of the building he had just entered. He watched colored light seep from the tiny doorway onto his skin. Small plastic figures trailed nearly around the perimeter. Part of the wall in front of him seemed to recede into darkness, but it was solid when he approached. He turned again to the miniature building. The lights continued to dim and saturate the room. Then he saw movement.

"Sir?"

The speaker was dressed in a dark suit with no tie, a triangular silhouette cinched at the waist by a tactical belt.

"Excuse me, sir?" the bouncer repeated. "Can you read?"

He nodded. The speaker indicated the wall opposite:

GET DOWN OR GET OUT

A flashlight emerged from the bouncer's coat sleeve. It took some time before the bouncer could clench the end of the long handle.

* * *

Outside, the wind intensified, carrying the night's last noises. He pushed against it, searching for a cab.

The street narrowed between lengths of chain-link. Arrows marked a detour around the latest construction. The plywood path tilted loosely as he walked. He felt his eyes strain into a growing obscurity. He steadied himself by clutching at the surrounding rungs and felt something soft against his knuckles. The fencing here had been reinforced with cloth mesh. He peered through a tear in the material into an empty street.

He followed irregularly spaced bulbs down a corridor, where shadows seemed to move at an approaching turn. He joined the back of a line waiting under a cavernous archway. The line snaked far ahead before rising over a wide flight of steps. The steps led to a platform where those waiting spread out, occasionally looking over the edge. From his place on the platform, he saw a second platform rising in the distance opposite. The faces there were indistinct. He pushed his way to the front. As he craned his neck for a better view, a figure on the opposite platform matched his movements. The features edged by the dimness overhead were his own.

The figure's face was lost now among seated silhouettes. On his side, the gathering crowd shifted more tightly around him. He waited. At any moment, the face would reemerge. He would be looking. And he would know.

The Devil and the Dairy Princess

The Well at Founders Grove

Many critics, seeking a precedent for the work of novelist Clarence Randolph Winthrop, cite the fictional topographies of Anderson's Winesburg or Faulkner's Yoknapatawpha. The more discerning suggest a kinship with Joyce's Dublin, which can purportedly be reconstructed, block by block, from the Irish master's penultimate fiction. Winthrop was arguably even more fastidious in rendering the history of Avernus, the American province traced by the author from settlement to suburb in his best-known work. Whereas Joyce restricted himself to a single day, Winthrop plotted over centuries. The cumulative effect of all fifteen Avernus novels is odd, disquieting, and often moving. In the 1910 of *Avernus Road*—just before he encounters the motorcar carrying the disoriented retinue of film actress Lilly Dawes, whose arrival precipitates the subsequent story—a farmer digs a hole for a fence post. The narrator is describing the slice of pickaxe into rich loam when, shunted somehow through an intervening clause, the reader emerges on the same square of earth, first trod by bison, then by the bare feet of the continent's first human inhabitants, and then by the hooves of Spanish horses. The rhythm of their footfalls is resumed by the sift and pull of the pick, attendant now on the farmer's grave, one of the dozens needed in the wake of the influenza outbreak subsequently depicted in *Abide, Yon Horsemen!* It is impossible to convey in linear description the simultaneity evoked in Winthrop's prose, though many have tried.[1]

The sole exception within the Winthrop cycle is the five-by-five-foot square containing the town's central well, dug during the sweltering summer of 1630, when the fledgling outpost is making its last stand against drought and mutiny. An improvised congress of patriarchs and clergy, on the night of July 4, 1630—a date that would not escape evocation in later Avernus volumes—votes with near unanimity to disband the encampment and return to England with what little provisions can be gathered from the surrounding wilderness. The sole holdout is Pastor Nicholas Roark, whose humility will not allow outright opposition but whose idealism prompts abstention in the climactic vote. Roark retreats to his quarters, which do nothing to shelter him from the sodden air breaching his walls. He rises from the flameless pyre of his bed and goes outside. Apart from a ribbon of mist shrouding the tree line, there is nothing to draw the eye. Nevertheless, Roark is depicted searching the distance until he hits on something that alters his expression with the semblance of illumination. The narrator watches Roark retreat further and further into the wilderness until his pearly nightclothes fade between darkened trunks.

At least forty articles and two monographs have been devoted to the ellipsis that occurs between Roark's disappearance into the woods and the subsequent morning, when he emerges carrying a stone basin "laden with fresh water of the most crystalline sweetness."[2] Their salvation astonishes the colonists only slightly more than its disheveled

---

1. See, e.g., Collin Winchell, "Tropes of Time in the Avernus Cycle," *Modernist Narrative Review* 10 (1978): 243–277.
2. Clarence R. Winthrop, *The Clearing* (New York: Bassett Books, 1949), 379.

The Devil and the Dairy Princess

bearer, who is naked, soiled, and streaked with blood. He approaches each witness in turn and compels them to drink in pledge to the land where fate has rooted them, which, from this day forward, will be known as Avernus. The people form a sacramental line before the pastor. The asterisk of a passing bird punctuates the sky overhead, unseen by the relieved pilgrims.

Sifting through the arcana of Winthrop scholarship, one is confronted by a legitimate question: Why, in an otherwise studiously constructed fictional community, would the author avoid direct depiction of such a thematically central location with what appears to be an equal compulsion? If one were to map Avernus over the centuries, the well would persist as a tile of blank parchment at the center of the burgeoning hamlet. Founders Grove is dedicated in *Rage and Resilience* during a ceremony of commemoration and solace for those awaiting the return of kin from the European theater in 1944. The grove's location is vaguely glossed as "skirting the path traced by Pastor Roark's nocturnal pilgrimage into the dawn of Avernus."[3] The omission is all the more bizarre if one considers that Founders Grove is the setting of numerous events central to the town's history: seven weddings; four adulterous assignations; eleven nocturnal escapes for parts unknown; twenty-seven soliloquies waxing on the contingencies that have brought the respective speaker to his or her good, bad, or indifferent fortune; dozens of family picnics; and six recoveries of lost children, including the orphan Emmanuel Lot, who departs for a prestigious clerkship in Washington, DC, at the conclusion of *The Turning Tide*, the final Avernus novel, published in 1978.

Winthrop, by then a taciturn octogenarian, claimed he was ready for retirement. In his last published interview, he was asked if this meant the Avernus cycle was complete. His reply was cryptic: "The design of Avernus has always been clear in my mind, from the first sentence to the last. That design is nearly complete."[4]

---

3. Clarence R. Winthrop, *Rage and Resilience* (New York: Bassett Books, 1961), 101.
4. Anthony Stillman, "American Master Still Has Stories to Tell," *Creative Writers Monthly* 18, (September 1988): 47.

On December 14, 1994, several hours into celebrating his ninety-sixth birthday, Winthrop retreated to his study with a plate of apple crisp à la mode; he asked his housekeeper, Angela Turley, to fetch a fresh bottle of brandy from the wine cellar. Turley, on returning with the bottle and a tumbler, heard murmuring from behind the closed door. She shifted her tray with bristling forbearance, discerning impatience in the muffled summons. She found Winthrop with his back to the door, probing weakly at a shelf overhead. Turley asked if she should get the stepladder; Winthrop's face, turned in reply, was smeared with apple and vanilla ice cream, his lips angled spastically over the ragged monosyllable that would be his final utterance. At some point between collapse and extreme unction, Turley wrested a sheaf of creased papers from the author's fisted hand. She smoothed the sheets against the blotter of Winthrop's desk, more out of habit than any expectation of his return. At the top of the first page, in a neat hand Winthrop only used for final versions sent to his typist, the manuscript was marked, "The Well at Founders Grove."

There followed, in the subsequent six months, the most contentious period of American criticism in recent memory. Winthrop, a widower, left everything to his son, Daniel; Josephine, his estranged elder daughter, had never forgiven her father for the love he immolated on the altar of Art. Daniel came to a verbal agreement with the English Department at Hereford, his father's alma mater, for possession of the Winthrop papers. Within a week, the president of Brook Falls University called a press conference to announce the delivery of all forty-seven file boxes by Daniel Winthrop himself. In the sparsely filled auditorium, it was hard to miss Josephine Winthrop's attendance. An investment consultant based in Boston and an alumnus of Brook Falls, Josephine began her stint on the university's board of trustees the following summer.

Colleagues nationwide were too curious to be indignant for very long. The first annual Clarence Winthrop Society Conference was hastily scheduled and organized around the one-year anniversary of the author's death. Within a month of the announcement and call for papers, registration was sold out, and bed-and-breakfasts were filling up as far away as North Adams and Pittsfield. A captive audience for the entire weekend was guaranteed with the scheduling of a plenary on Winthrop's last work—including personal reminiscences by Angela Turley—for the concluding Sunday morning. Brook Falls faculty with access to the archive insisted that the papers were still being reviewed and that there was no confirmed existence of new fiction by Winthrop, Avernus-related or otherwise. But it took little time for rumor and anecdote to promise the revelation of Winthrop's last masterpiece.

Moderator Theodore Meade looked nervous as he assumed the middle chair on the dais. The assembled crowd, which occupied well over half of Chapman Auditorium, burst into spirited applause as Meade, an associate professor of American literature and film studies, cleared his throat, and announced the start of the plenary. He apologized for the absence of Professor Hubert Crosby, Brook Falls's resident Winthropist and chair of the ad hoc committee organizing the contents of Winthrop's papers. He introduced Angela Turley—who was greeted with a standing ovation—and invited her to share some reminiscences of her late employer. Turley, unaccustomed to audiences larger than Winthrop and the occasional neighbor or visiting luminary, stumbled through several familiar episodes and eccentricities: the author's sweet tooth, his fondness for bird-watching, his almost equal fondness for the squirrels that regularly invaded the stores of seed he used to lure wild birds to his windows, and his insistence on beginning and completing his works in longhand in order to feel the integrity building, word by word, of a nascent narrative.

A professor in one of the front rows—whose rudeness is alternately attributed to coming from either New York City or Berkeley—took advantage of this opening to ask about the discovery of "The Well at Founders Grove." Turley retold the events of the previous December, augmented by a new detail that prompted a volley of impatient queries from the restless audience: As she straightened the crinkled manuscript recovered from Winthrop's grasp, Turley happened to browse not just the title but the concluding page as well, which was scored by a downward slash of black ink doubtless corresponding to the moment the author was stricken.

What did she mean by conclusion? asked an eager Americanist at the back of the auditorium.

Just what she had said. The manuscript ended and was subsequently scored by the writer's fountain pen, the only instrument he ever used to copy out his final versions.

Several in the audience stood in response. With all due respect, began a jetlagged assistant professor from the Pacific Northwest, Turley had just contradicted herself. She initially described the manuscript concluding with the aforementioned slash. Now she was saying that the manuscript was finished and that, just before popping a celebratory toffee—not to be glib—the onset of the fatal attack caused Winthrop to lose control of his writing hand and slash incoherently at the last page. Which was it?

Turley could not be sure.

Did she, perhaps, notice the presence of punctuation at the end of the last line? A period, say, or an exclamation mark?

Ending with a bang, not a whimper, mused aloud a semiotician from downstate.

Turley drank impassively from her water glass as she waited for the chuckling in the room to ebb. She had graduated from college, she observed once the crowd was silent. Nothing as prestigious as the institution that likely sired her esteemed interlocutor. But she knew her letters.

Sensing the edge in Turley's voice, a member of the Brook Falls senior faculty reminded those assembled of the good fortune they had in access not only to the poignant reminiscences of Ms. Turley but also the author's originals. Heads turned expectantly to the dais where Theodore Meade leaned reluctantly toward his microphone. He assured his audience that all their questions would be answered eventually, but the truth was that no manuscript for "The Well at Founders Grove" had been recovered from the cache delivered by Daniel Winthrop. Furthermore, Professor Crosby's absence prevented the insights likely to be gleaned from his expertise.

The subsequent outcry and accusations of bad faith obscured the distant sound of sirens. The prospect of an early lunch—the hosting institution's treat—did little to quell disappointment. As Meade tried to stem a mass departure for the Albany airport, a conference volunteer handed him a folded note. He saw his home number scrawled over the

The Devil and the Dairy Princess

top of the pink carbon, along with instructions to return immediately to his house on Avenue of the Elms.

When Meade would tell the story later, he would always linger on the anxiety of the drive back. He would depict himself agonizing at every crosswalk and jaywalking pedestrian, wondering what prompted such a stark summons from his wife. Was Sarah having another panic attack? (Her doctor had yet to find an anxiety medication without vexing side effects.) Had his daughter Alice toddled into an unsecured cabinet of lethal cleaning agents? In fact, all he could think of on his short drive to the outskirts of Brook Falls was the vanity of his profession, reputations rising and falling on the location and contents of a faded luminary's dusty manuscripts, parsed ad nauseam by cliquish specialists who, having lost their imaginations early in graduate school, were determined to crush what little was left in the literary landscape. He stopped to let a senior student in his American Naturalism seminar cross toward the bookstore on Water Street. She didn't seem to recognize him from beneath the low angle of her baseball cap. He watched the acronym of his home institution sway in taut arcs on the back of her sweatpants. He was roused to self-awareness by two simultaneous perceptions: the blare of car horns behind him and the widening funnel of smoke rising from the direction of his house.

Meade followed the smoke to his driveway, where his wife and daughter stood watching the scramble of emergency vehicles across the street. Flames were visible through the second-floor windows of his colleague, Hubert Crosby. He ignored his wife's warnings and crossed to a waiting ambulance. Crosby was prone on a stretcher, but on seeing Meade, he began to howl from behind his oxygen mask. He caught hold of Meade's sleeve and fogged the clear plastic with the effort to speak. The EMTs, now attending to a firefighter knocked unconscious, failed to intervene when Meade, discerning the word *mask*, slid the restraint aside.

Crosby smiled with what at first appeared to be relief. But it only took a moment for Meade to place the expression more accurately, from administrative meetings where the two happened to sit side by side or the occasional drink they shared at the Woodchuck and Starling on Main Street: the exhausted leer of a man betrayed by absurdities too hilarious to leave unremarked and too pervasive to redress or escape. He seemed to mumble to himself as smoke thickened around them; only when it completely obscured the surrounding block, leaving the voice alone as landmark and beacon, did Meade discern the rhythm of his colleague's recitation, snatches of familiar text punctuating an emergent and terrible silence, like moonlight stippling the contours of a dark expanse. He ignored the effort of breathing to listen.

* * *

Winthrop was notoriously reticent about his writing process. Speculation usually attributed this to superstition or a vain desire to mask the banality of routine with the mystery more appropriate to his stature. The sole published exception is an essay that appeared posthumously in a volume celebrating the centennial of Jorge Luis Borges's birth.[5] Winthrop's meandering foray into nonfictional prose—which, if anything, demonstrates his aptness for longer forms—begins as a meditation on Borges's blindness and concludes by asserting that all writers suffer a similar, albeit metaphorical, impairment. While resisting any special claims the writer may have over the doctor, the banker, or the engineer, Winthrop argues that no other profession is more singularly dedicated to making something out of nothing. Even the painter has his paints, the sculptor his clay or stone, but the writer has no such tangible medium in which to moor his incipient creation. A story is told word by word, letter by letter, the friction of pen on paper seeding the infinite night with feeble sparks. How many would be subsumed before the flicker of a single flame? And what mute shapes would be revealed in its wavering light?

* * *

As Crosby, unmasked, completed Winthrop's vision, his memory now absorbed within its object of remembrance, Meade could not be sure if the smoke was rising or if he himself was falling. For if Winthrop

---

5. Clarence R. Winthrop, "On Blindness and Composition," in *A is for Aleph: An Abecedarian in Honor of Borges*, ed. Inez Menard (Santa Fe: Cíbola Press, 1999), 57–72.

had spent a lifetime stoking fires in the night, the surrounding darkness had not been dispelled so much as concentrated into smaller and smaller spaces that seethed now in the words from Crosby's tongue. Winthrop had, in fact, not spent his last two decades composing an epilogue but rather the substance of his story, which had as its prologue the fifteen preceding volumes. Avernus past, present, and future emerged with portentous coherence appending the nullity of its origins, delineating a cancellation only deferred by the miracle of Pastor Roark. The generations that thrived on water from a hollow in the earth had made a covenant with both the land and its vacancy, fulfilled at last by its creator, who had waited with geologic patience to pull taut the strings that threaded fiction with actuality.

Meade struggled to breathe. The smoke formed a solid coil against his chest. He heard voices nearby. He surrendered to the restraining arm of the technician whose partner wrested the silent stretcher from his grasp.

Professor Hubert Crosby succumbed to smoke inhalation within minutes of his hospitalization. The fire at his home on Avenue of the Elms has been declared an accident.

All forty-seven boxes of the Winthrop papers were recovered from the former home of Hubert Crosby in pristine condition. The manuscript alleged to exist by Angela Turley has yet to be found.

Citing inadequate facilities for proper storage, the Louis Herbert Rare Book Collection at Brook Falls University has offered the Winthrop papers to numerous scholarly archives in the United States and abroad, with shipping and insurance provided at the university's expense. Interest thus far has been negligible.

The Abbreviated Life of
Whitney Bascombe

Whitney Bascombe was one of the last of her kind—at least in the more developed American hemisphere—to be subjected to that brutal school of parenting in which actualities were starkly acknowledged. Her antecedents, who settled the Great Plains in houses of sod or battled natives on their inevitable progress west, were pragmatists by necessity; survival required a singularity of purpose that left no room for fancy or compassion.

The pragmatism of Whitney's mother could arguably be attributed to similar circumstances. Abandoned by Whitney's father in the second trimester of her pregnancy, Sheila Bascombe carried to term through double shifts at her local House of Tapas. What would have been the lying-in for her forbears she spent on her feet during a week of promoting the franchise's new brunch menu; she disguised her condition using loose garments that had the added advantage of curtailing harassment by her unscrupulous supervisor. She had just put in an order for an Iberian omelet with a side of maple bacon churros when she could no longer dissemble the pain of incipient contractions. Her water broke as she clutched the serape of the life-size Pancho Tortilla mascot that ushered "Caballeros" and "Damas" toward the restrooms. If she ever allowed herself a fear proportional to her circumstances, it was perhaps now, as she lost consciousness beneath Pancho's sleepy grin and polka-dot stubble. Had her mother's labor begun several years later, Whitney Bascombe would have been greeted by the possibly more propitious—and certainly more culturally sensitive—avian mascot Gary Gallo.

Whitney's own education began not much later, at the age of two and a half. Her mother had, by this point, settled into an indifferent marriage with an associate editor in the textbook division of Dumont and Dunn. Whitney's stepfather was an aspiring novelist, which is to say that his cultivation of others' words left him too exhausted to care when he managed to steal an hour or two for his own. Nevertheless, he had managed to take the manuscript of *Muses and Miscreants*—a fictionalized memoir of his years as an expatriate artist in Central and South America—through three and a half drafts. As extramarital activities go, those of Sheila's second husband were infinitely preferable to those of the first. She tolerated his blandness as a life partner and, at times, even sympathized with his frustration as an artist, but she never forgot the true purpose of long-term commitment: as credit against contingencies swarming just beyond the sphere of the predictable.

The toddler Whitney Bascombe's first encounter with this metaphysics occurred on returning with her mother to the family sedan after their weekly grocery run. She glanced over her shoulder from her berth in the foldout seat of a shopping cart. Her mother struggled with the capricious lock on the sedan's trunk, ignoring the pile of black and gray feathers that rippled feebly between the lines of their parking space. The girl recognized the shape of wings and a beak, but the neck seemed strangely elongated against the muddy pavement.

"Bird sleep?" asked Whitney.

Her mother looked down at the pigeon clumped at her feet. At last the trunk yielded. "Not asleep," she answered. "Dead." She began unloading the cart.

Whitney looked curiously at her mother. "When bird wake up?" she asked.

"Never," replied her mother. She kicked the corpse aside as she handled a particularly heavy paper bag. Whitney watched the sodden feathers roll away and stop against the concrete edge of an island. The wind picked up, severing the remains of a wing from the collapsed body. The cart, nearly empty, shook loose underneath.

"Why?" wailed Whitney, as she watched her mother slowly retreat in the forceful gust.

Her mother shut the trunk and arrested the cart with two fingers thrust through the wide metal mesh. "Who knows?" she replied, brusquely lifting her daughter from her seat.

Whitney's cries began to draw the attention of nearby customers exiting the store. "Take bird home!" she screamed.

Sheila Bascombe set her daughter gently down and wiped the tears streaking her cheeks. "Dead things don't go home," she said.

"Take bird home!" Whitney insisted.

Sheila now grasped her daughter firmly by the waist. She looked intently at her pale blue eyes, the only trace that remained of her father. "Dead stay," she said, pointing at the broken bird. "Alive home. Are you dead or alive?"

Whitney studied the pigeon; she felt no less sad or disgusted by the corruption that had burst suddenly from its feathers. But she remembered now it was Friday, which was tomato soup, Tater Bite, and fish stick day. She swallowed in anticipation, and her saliva absorbed the cold metallic taste of rain. "Alive," she answered, allowing herself to be lifted into the car.

*　*　*

The origins of Whitney Bascombe's uncompromising instinct for survival are not hard to trace; its rhetorical and aesthetic manifestations, by contrast, are less clearly foreshadowed. She was by all accounts a typical child, with a not unexpected record of demerits for talking in class and passing notes. Her physiognomy betrayed none of the severity that would mark her career as an editor. Ironically, if the Dickensian storyteller were to look for the future bane of the digressive or imprecise, he or she would inevitably look to Whitney's younger half-sister Iris. Born two years into Sheila's remarriage, Iris possessed none of the softness or ostentation of her namesake. Whitney was always the prettier sister, with a roundness to her face and body that in the child was adorable, and in the young girl mildly disquieting. The sisters lived together peaceably, Iris in hopeless emulation of Whitney, Whitney in the authority imparted by her unworthy adversary.

Whitney's editorial talents arose fully formed in her sophomore year of high school. Having procrastinated until the night before to begin a short story due the following morning in English, she spent several blank-faced hours before her computer screen before retreating downstairs, less for sustenance from the family's well-stocked refrigerator than for relief from her complete lack of ideas. She passed by her stepfather's study. The open door revealed that the desk light was still on. The study was not forbidden territory for the children; Whitney's original purpose, in fact, was quite innocent and responsible—her mother, having never relinquished her parsimonious caution, had instilled in her eldest a constant vigilance against waste of all kinds. She was about to extinguish the squandered light when she saw the latest version of her stepfather's manuscript; its rubber band fastening had been barely removed before Iris called down to be tucked in. Whitney began reading. Even at her age, she recognized the wooden dialogue and clumsy lyricism of the amateur. But beneath the excesses, she sensed a solid foundation of plot that could yet be salvaged with judicious pruning. She turned off the light, took the stack of penciled pages, and proceeded upstairs, pausing briefly to assure herself of the even breaths continuing from behind her parents' door.

By 5:48 the next morning—leaving her a mere twelve minutes to sneak down and replace the borrowed manuscript before the blare of her mother's alarm—Whitney had extracted her first published work from the rubble and scaffolding of her stepfather's novel. To call it plagiarism would be to overlook the delicacy and craft of her excisions.

One could just as well accuse the sculptor of stealing from the stone. And the young editor did make several changes to cover her tracks, transferring the action to Africa and changing the age, gender, and vocation of the first-person narrator from that of a twentysomething male apprentice artist to that of an orphaned teenage female trying to find herself. Ironically, these very changes, hastily inserted to imbue her work with a semblance of originality, undermined the intended effect. This was particularly noticeable in the central motif of the now rechristened "Song of the Hummingbird"—it is unclear whether the Latin American species described at length in the original would have existed "on the arid plains of Nairobi." Such questionable verisimilitude was lost, however, on Whitney's English teacher, who also served as faculty advisor for *The Beacon*; she recognized in her pupil's narrative distillation—nonetheless, at fifteen double-spaced pages, a veritable epic by the standards of student composition—just the kind of precocious insight lacking in the pages of the campus newspaper.

The story took up three and a half pages in the tabloid's final spring semester issue and was awarded first prize in fiction in the school's annual creative writing competition. The award assembly included readings by the winner in each category. Whether Whitney suffered any crisis of conscience as she approached the podium is unclear from the available record. Her mother, seated next to her husband in the auditorium's third row, center, dissembled her disappointment that the fiction prize was paid not in cash but credit for more books. Due to the length of her winning entry, Whitney could only read a portion of her piece, but it only took the first page for her stepfather to recognize the source of her inspiration. He vacillated wordlessly as he listened between disbelief, denial, and a rage he allowed himself only in dreams or the most removed of solitudes. The parallels with grief and mourning are not incidental; for, as he listened to his experiences emerge sparsely fledged but muscular in their denuded essence, he apprehended the frailty of his stylistic excesses and the vanity that prompted his sustaining of them. For the rest of his life, he would wield his blue pencil—and, for a time, a digital pen—with competence and occasional flair. But he never again resumed more creative endeavors. Neither did he ever tarnish the occasion of his stepdaughter's earliest triumph.

The Devil and the Dairy Princess

Even if one could circumvent the legal barriers involved, our subject's undergraduate records would be forever lost to the diligent researcher, victims of a freakish electrical storm and her institution's spendthrift investment in data preservation. She had to have pursued graduate study at some point in order to compete successfully for editorial work, if not at the entry level, then certainly when she interviewed for the ambitious entrepreneurs who founded the Consolidated Media Consortium in 1999. In the Fall 1997 edition of the *Horn and Laurel* alumni magazine, the master's candidate seen scowling in profile at one of the Romulus Pitkin Library's new high-speed search terminals strongly resembles Whitney Bascombe; that said, the more one looks at the image, the more the resemblance seems to slip into any number of possibilities. The caption writer, perhaps more concerned with detailing the specifications of the larger, high-resolution screen and simplified graphic menu, omitted the identity of the student pictured. If Whitney was a graduate student, she was not interested in building a recognized reputation within her discipline. She is completely absent from departmental and university newsletters where aspiring scholars plant the first shallow roots of their curricula vitae.

This does not mean, however, she was not doing her part for the profession. Word-of-mouth in the student dormitories alluded more and more frequently to "the Harrow," an otherwise unidentified writing tutor at the Orson Revelle Center for Student Competencies. At the time of Whitney Bascombe's likely graduate matriculation, the Center would have paid tutors $10 per hour of student consultation, a not inconsiderable addition to the university's notoriously stingy teaching and research stipends. Bascombe would have enjoyed the extra income, but she would have also welcomed a challenge she deemed worthy of her distinct talent. If she failed to distinguish herself in the literary seminars required for an advanced degree, it was not for lack of preparation or comprehension. If anything, she would have found the language of her presumed discipline maddening for its often needless inflation of ideas that, expressed concisely, would have revealed the pedestrian insights at their core. The abstract of a typical journal article alone would have been vulnerable to her ruthless quest for concision. Boredom and need would have led her inevitably to the underground economy supporting student dereliction. The anxious athlete or tearful sorority pledge might have paid several times the going rate for a ghostwriter on assignments neglected until the last possible minute. Soon enough, a Whitney Bascombe could be doing brisk business.

Her earliest customers, however, were put off by her trademark aesthetic. She ignored page counts, condensing scribbled notes and typed outlines into explications, arguments, analyses, and critiques several pages shy of the assigned minimum. "Where's the rest of it?" clients demanded, some still affected by the extra night of revelry afforded by the Harrow. "I used everything you gave me," the Harrow would respond to the bleariness veiled beneath drawn hoods and visors. Her clients might have demanded refunds, but Bascombe would have already spent them—payment was due before services rendered, cash only. Most, under the circumstances, were just relieved to have something to turn in.

Bascombe flourished in her new vocation. She was frequently spotted—alone or with a date—at dining and entertainment establishments well beyond the means of her colleagues: the Billings Brothers Steakhouse, Imperial Thai, Heure Flâneur (continental cuisine), Uqbar ($7 cover weeknights, $10 cover weekends, two-drink minimum).

She lived as she worked. She had no patience for the rituals of courtship, which for her were the romantic equivalent of a compound sentence, sluggish with conjunctions and unnecessary clauses. Her affairs were infrequent and brief, but they condensed months, even years, of routine to the most piercing syllables uttered from beds, bunks, desktops, and shower stalls. A fellow doctorate—strangely enough, a Marxist and gender critic in the department of American Studies—managed to possess her for most of a three-day weekend at the beginning of the winter quarter. Giddy from satiety and lack of sleep, he proposed marriage, using the only ring at hand to seal his intent—his undergraduate class ring, bearing the cumbersome crest of his East Coast alma mater. She consented to its placement on her hand; it rolled loosely at the thickest knuckle. Gently, he propped the crest right side up and promised to save for a proper engagement ring. She laid her

The Devil and the Dairy Princess

other hand over his and smiled gravely. She needed time, she said. He nodded. She kissed him and said she was hungry. He offered to take her out to brunch after a quick shower. He left her, one of his ragged T-shirts skirting her thighs as she cooed into the pillows about blueberry pancakes. When he emerged from the bathroom, she was gone. The bed was made, his shirt neatly folded in its customary drawer. The only sign that he had not dreamed the entire weekend was the ring, which she had left as her only reply on the blank bedding. He knew her name but nothing else. By the time he began his inquiries around the Department of Rhetoric, Languages, and Literatures, she had all but dropped out, her name no better than an alias to the department's impassive administrative staff.

It was around this time that Bascombe arrived at her cubicle in the Revelle Center and found someone already waiting for her. She tried to hide her annoyance; she had no appointments for her first scheduled hour of tutoring and was looking forward to finishing a volume of Kawabata she had been enjoying between clients. Her current client was unusually polite, standing to introduce himself. She could smell his lemon aftershave as they shook hands. His cufflinks and pin-striped blue suit marked him as a business student, doubtless one who could pay quarterly tuition from the proceeds of a single job—or even personal savings. She became instantly solicitous and asked how she could be of service.

This client, however, was not a client at all—Theodore Hopper had already completed both a JD and an MBA at another institution, one she had never heard of. Her editorial skills had come highly praised to the attention of his business partners. Hopper was essentially here to advertise himself. In response to her undisguised skepticism, he withdrew a small silver case from his coat pocket and extracted one of his business cards. He excused himself to scribble an address on the blank side of the card; the gold-plated barrel of his fountain pen was etched with an angular insignia that was illegible viewed from where she sat. He and his partners were looking to expand their operations. If she was interested, she was to be at the address tomorrow evening for an informational orientation. He expressed his sincere hope that he would see her there before collecting his things and departing with a polite nod.

At this point, she might have noticed a hint of flirtation in the entrepreneur's proposition. This prospect, however, was outweighed in Bascombe's mind by the chance to finally abandon her studies altogether, which had become nothing more than unprofitable intervals between paying jobs.

The following evening, she arrived a few minutes before seven. It was a part of the city she had never been to before, located just east of the city's fashionable lower downtown. Behind townhouse facades spray-painted to resemble New York City punk dens or festooned with the crumbling statuary of an imagined bohemian Paris, abandoned warehouses crouched ominously beneath intermittent streetlamps. She felt the lightness of her purse as she turned away from the buzz of weeknight drinking. She had forgotten to replenish her pepper spray; the heaviest object now in her possession was a collapsible umbrella, which she took out. Opened, it was a feeble shield that swayed cumbersomely in front of her. Cursing, she folded the umbrella into its cloth case but kept the handle extended. With her blunt lance, she continued into the darkness. Silhouettes seemed to peer at her from illuminated windows several stories up. Three blocks in, she saw light slanting onto the pavement. Wavering shapes cut back and forth across what she could now see was an open doorway. Not until she recognized her visitor from the day before, a small crowd gathering behind him in ranks of folding chairs, did she unclench her hands.

"Right on time," Hopper said. He pointed toward the complimentary hors d'oeuvres with his clipboard.

She had barely taken a seat with her wine and canapés when the lights began to dim and a screen was lowered in front of the assembled guests. It would not occur to her until later how the screen appeared from a bare ceiling fixed with fluorescent tubes. The film began and ended without credits. Slowly, the screen came to life with the first in a series of questions, definitions, interjections, and historical dates: "HOW DO WE KNOW WHAT WE KNOW?" The letters dissolved into the candlelit cell of a monk, patiently transcribing text in a dead language onto a blank scroll. The reconstruction's accuracy was questionable, the monk's earnest expression at his desk amateurish and overdone, but the performance was enough to elicit hysterics from

Bascombe and others scattered throughout the improvised auditorium. She cupped her hand quickly to her mouth in response to several irritated whispers and managed the rest of the screening in silence.

If one could say that the orientation film had a plot, it somehow involved the evolution of the brain; the supplanting of oral with written culture; the approaching millennium; the use of hypnosis to treat physical and psychosomatic disorders; the universal centrality of sacred texts in all major religions; inscrutable petroglyphs in the Andes and in southeast Asia predating Egyptian civilization by several thousand years; cryptography during and after World War II; the pattern and relative strength of synaptic activity elicited by pronouncing or hearing certain common and less common letter combinations; the often neglected role that sound, taste, touch, and smell have in the learning process ("THE JOY OF SENSE"); the successful trial of specially designed pictographic cards in preparing a group of high school students for college-level exams; the unsuccessful trial of a similar second group that studied longer, using full texts instead of pictographs for the same exam; space travel; national security; a global network of information rising from the ashes of Alexandria; and *Homo Cerebrus,* an artist's projection of the "all brain" macrocephalic superbeings representing the pinnacle of human evolution.

Bascombe was impressed. Had she been asked for a narrative of what had been represented onscreen, she would have likely not been able to provide one beyond the foregoing fragmentary list. But it was impossible for the uninitiated to appreciate the coherence of what had just unfolded. She would later liken it to a long and particularly intense conversation at a party in which intoxication actually sharpened perception, rather than impairing it. She could parse every logical twist and turn of phrase as it was spoken; she could sense an order underpinning even the conversation's most far-flung digression. But if you asked her the next morning what had transpired, she would be unable to recreate the profundity of her impressions. This would do nothing, however, to undercut her sense that this night had changed everything.

She found Hopper at a long table set up near the door. He seemed to avoid eye contact as he gave her one of the company's application portfolios. She wondered what accounted for his coolness. As she left, she was struck by his resemblance to the monk from the orientation film. She hoped she had not ruined her chances as she made her way home to fill out the application. Two weeks after sending off her materials in the enclosed postage-paid envelope, she was called by a Consolidated Media Consortium representative and offered a job in the recently opened Research Division not far from the site of her orientation. Bascombe had scored so highly on her candidate questionnaire that the hiring board had decided to hire without the usual personal interview. Bascombe took little time to consider the offer, according to available evidence: There is no record of her ever completing a course of graduate study.

She had no idea what to expect on first arriving at the glass monolith that was then CMC headquarters on the following Monday. But after the tour of the Research Division's fifth- and sixth-floor offices—her elevator card afforded her access to only these floors—and the invitation to nachos after work at the conveniently located Cecil's Tavern, Bascombe realized that she had finally found her calling. Every morning, her desk would be piled with several volumes that needed processing by the end of business that day. The volumes themselves had little apparent relation apart from the frail rubber band binding them loosely together. There were outmoded primers on fashionable dances, manuals for sending and interpreting floral arrangements, guides to the flora and fauna of now nonexistent countries, crumbling almanacs from centuries past. She was to take these volumes and encode them into one of fourteen discipline-specific databases using CMC software that distilled pages of print into a single screen of digital data. A boon for libraries and archives with limited shelf space, the CMC electronic collections resembled the outmoded card catalog, with one very important difference: searching the latter, one only accessed the card representing the desired text, while the former yielded the text itself, rendered to its pictographic essence using simple sentences and mnemonic icons. The full text—scanned on a separate floor—was available for a modest fee, which would go toward preservation of the print original in the CMC's state-of-the-art, climate-controlled archive on the outskirts of Temecula, California.

The Devil and the Dairy Princess

She enjoyed her work, especially after a second cup of French-pressed coffee from her floor's small but well-stocked kitchenette. She began with wrinkled, fading, and cracked volumes; by the end of the day, she had tamed this unwieldy assemblage of knowledge into several screens of palatable information. Her stack of materials was usually the first to be replaced on the trolley for transfer to the archive; the clerk who collected her trolley would linger to chat and admire her speed. Mindful of the cameras discreetly housed overhead, she would respond with few words—perhaps a quick, neutral smile—before opening her purse for inspection on the way to the elevators. The occasional new or even old hire would pause in his or her digest to run a hand along a torn binding, lift the frail tissue protecting an etching or daguerreotype, become absorbed by a stray paragraph. It was a rare but unfortunate employee who, fascinated by a volume's arcane intricacy, yielded it with reluctance to the archive cart or even attempted to sneak it out in a discreet pocket. Bascombe, however, was never reprimanded in the quietly maintained record of employee conduct. She was soon promoted to Serials, Compendiums, and Miscellanies.

Speculation has no place in the responsible biography, but there are times when the standard of discretion must give way to the higher standard of accuracy. Her performance to the contrary, Whitney Bascombe was not a machine. She had at last established the kind of life she had dreamed of during the lean times of scholarly apprenticeship. If one subscribes to the notion of hierarchies marking one's progress through life, her achievement of basic subsistence and domestic comfort prompted needs of a higher order. One cannot deny the human element that embroiders even the starkest of circumstances with intimacies, affections, desires. It would not be long before Theodore Hopper, her original liaison to the company, stopped by her cubicle. He apologized for not being more available during her first months of employment and offered to take her to lunch. When a sudden conflict made lunch impossible, he asked about dinner.

"Unless that would make you uncomfortable," he said, his tone at once coy and anxious at being possibly misunderstood.

"Uncomfortable?" she replied. "Why would that make me uncomfortable, Mr. Hopper?"

"Dinner is usually the date meal, isn't it?" he said.

Dinner turned out to be Mediterranean takeout; their original reservation was lost after instinct overcame propriety at the threshold of Bascombe's apartment. She kicked aside clothes scattered in the wake of their urgency and maneuvered the bulging delivery bag to the kitchen. They said little to each other as they filled their plates with gyros, hummus, and tabbouleh. Hopper asked about her life before CMC; she obliged his curiosity with an unusually honest if characteristically attenuated personal history between bites of stuffed grape leaves. This is not to say she felt for Hopper any differently than her previous partners. But she recognized in him a common pliancy of attraction; already, as he remarked on her excellent choice of merlot and mimicked a particularly irritating coworker for her amusement, she sensed him preparing a charming but definitive exit. Their repartee now was no deeper than that of commuters filling a lull between trains.

"So what do you like most about being gainfully employed?" he asked, emptying the last of the wine into their glasses.

"The benefits, definitely," she said. She paused at her choice of words. They laughed nervously, looking at each other. "I mean, you don't get dental for reading Ben Jonson."

Hopper nodded. "And maternity leave. We're more generous than most."

Bascombe fixed him now with a hint of annoyance. "Why would I be interested in that?"

He sipped more of his wine. "I didn't mean anything by it. I was just—"

"What about you?" she continued. "When are you planning to take time off to raise a family?"

He smirked. "Someday."

"Really? You don't strike me as the type."

Hopper shaped his features into a semblance of offense. He set his drink down and pulled lightly at the cincture of her bathrobe. "Marriage and family are a sound investment. Cheaper than a nursing home." He lowered his hands to her waist. "Don't you care about the future?"

"The future is for suckers."

He was looking at her now with unexpected intensity. "You really mean that, don't you?"

She hesitated before answering. "I don't know. I guess . . . I guess I do." She began to undo her robe but stopped. "You're not one of *those* guys, are you?"

"What guys?"

"The ones who are hot and heavy the night before, but needy bitches the morning after."

He parted the robe with one quick tug. She was naked underneath. He ran his palm along the inside of her thigh. "I believe in destiny," he said, "but there's nothing romantic about it." He led her back to bed.

Her suspicions were groundless. On Monday, they shared the same elevator. Hopper asked with perfunctory interest about the rest of her weekend, but his eyes roamed as she answered, settling on the toxic orange tresses of the newest hire in Periodicals. He was unctuously solicitous as he introduced her to Bascombe and asked the girl—their youngest hire to date, fresh from the local university's bachelor's program in Digital Media—how she was doing. Later, Bascombe entered the kitchenette for more coffee and found him chatting over Danish with an executive she had never seen before. She was mindful that her work required maintaining the spirit, if not the substance, of professionalism. She decided to say hello. But as she turned with her refilled cup, she heard the whispering behind her stop; both men seemed to leer at her, slouching with invitation. On her way out, she hoisted her cup and bid them a loud good morning. The nearest camera caught the toast and her exaggerated grin, but missed the raised middle finger obscured by the coffee. The men's expressions remained unchanged.

She returned home to find a message from her mother. Her stepfather had suffered an episode of aphasia at work; his condition was stable, but he was being hospitalized overnight for observation. She offered to fly out immediately to be with her parents. One should not marvel at the sincerity of the offer. The Bascombes were practical women, but this should not be mistaken for callousness. A conscientious economy of acquisition and debt underpinned their instinct for survival. Her stepfather had supported them both with more than they had ever needed. It was time now for his credit to be redeemed. At this early stage, the blood clot could have affected any number of mental faculties and bodily functions that would now be the responsibility of his caregivers. Neither woman flinched as they looked forward to years of incontinence, special diets, and rehabilitation. They would do what was necessary for the remainder of his natural life, not out of love but obligation, stark as the calculus of a monthly utility. One could hope for better. One could suffer worse.

He awoke the next morning with a slur in his voice, some loss of short-term memory, and an impatience with sentences of two or more clauses in length. Despite this, his doctors considered him lucky; he was otherwise unaffected and sent home later that day. The rest and rehabilitation prescribed could be supervised by Whitney's mother and her half-sister, who lived with her husband less than an hour away.

Whitney checked in regularly on his progress. The speech therapist was tough, but good. His memory and language comprehension improved at a remarkable rate. The impediment in his speech lasted through Thanksgiving, but by the time she called about Christmas, it was barely noticeable over the phone. He noted down her flight information, reading it back slowly but accurately.

Christmas being a family holiday, there were numerous roles required of her in various seasonal traditions: as grudging babysitter for the children of her half-sister and several cousins as they finished their shopping; as object lesson of the indignities suffered by those forsaking the matrimonial sacrament ("Whitney, dear," Aunt Peg, her stepfather's sister, would cluck over her pearls and double chin, "are you *still* living in that awful studio apartment with the broken water heater?"); as grateful recipient of questionably stylish garments, never quite her size and inevitably lacking a gift receipt for easy return. She was also the table setter and announcer for Christmas dinner, a duty she had fulfilled since childhood, when she brought the entire living room to silence with indignant cries of boredom and hunger. This year, she was no less efficient but much more discreet. Having finished the place settings, she approached each group in the living room and quietly ushered them toward the table. Her stepfather was in his recliner by the fireplace, his eyes intent on a large white card. She looked over his shoulder and saw his finger tracing the crisp type and multicolored icons of a Consolidated Media Consortium digest. She recognized several symbols in the right margin: *history, birth, union*. "Dad," she asked, "where did you get that?"

He looked up, but on seeing her, he appeared too startled to speak. His stare was so vacant that for a moment she suspected a sudden regression and was about to alert her mother. Iris's daughter skipped back into the living room. "Grandpa," she said. "Mom says dinner's getting cold." He immediately rose from his seat and followed the girl toward the food, taking the card with him.

In the kitchen, her mother was filling a second gravy boat. "Mom," Whitney said. "Dad was acting funny in the living room."

"How so?"

"He was reading this card. It looked like—"

"That's nothing," she answered, wiping away a dribble. "The therapist gave him those."

"He has more?"

"She calls them memory cards. They help him not to get confused. Iris, can you—"

"Mom."

Sheila Bascombe looked at her eldest daughter and smiled. "Oh, it's you. I guess I could use some of those cards myself. Would you please?" she asked, holding the gravy out with one hand while shutting a burner off with the other.

Whitney was too busy surviving the holiday to dwell on the incident at dinner. She spent the New Year fighting a flu and searching for her friends at the city's elaborate outdoor fireworks display. Despite the widely publicized fact that this was the false millennium, the city had gone forward with elaborate plans to mark the start of the year 2000. At midnight, she watched rockets and fluorescent stars streak overhead, her friends nowhere in sight. The chill that had prickled her throughout the day settled into a dull throbbing. She took to her bed for the rest of the weekend.

On Monday, more or less recovered, she ran into Hopper near the elevators. She remembered her stepfather as the doors closed in front of them.

"I didn't know you were into therapy."

Hopper kept his eyes on the lit button of his floor. "What?"

"That must be new, right? The protocols say Consortium materials have to stay in this office."

"I don't know what you're talking about."

"Hey," she said, grasping his elbow. "I'm thanking you. Whatever you guys are doing, it's working great."

He looked at her as the doors opened. She saw the exhaustion in his expression harden into determined dismissal. He stepped out, saying nothing.

Hopper's coldness confused and irritated her, and she was slower with her daily quota of digests. She worked through lunch but still felt no hunger as she switched off her system terminal. This, she decided, was better than the feverish nights of the past weekend. The clerk who usually collected her parcel had not shown up; she was relieved to have one less thing between her and the exits as she placed the finished texts on the trolley.

Her apartment door was open when she arrived. Inside, two men were taking measurements with oddly shaped instruments while a third seemed to supervise and take notes. All three wore business suits. Bascombe, who had never seen them before, threatened to complain to her landlord; she had not been warned in advance of any work required on her apartment, certainly none that would interfere so late on a day when all she wanted was to spend a quiet evening at home. The supervisor nodded sympathetically but continued to scribble numbers and what looked like schematics onto his clipboard. He shook his head and asked for the time. One of his colleagues withdrew what looked like a miniature level from his pocket. The level seemed to have two transparent chambers; a radiant blue liquid flowed from one chamber to the other, drop by drop. The supervisor, who could apparently read the strange timepiece from where he stood, turned apologetically to Bascombe. "We are so very sorry," he said. "There were numerous appointments today, several of which took longer than expected."

Bascombe set down her purse and overcoat. "Did the landlord authorize this?" The three were again distracted, this time by the drapes next to the television. One of the men withdrew a silver rod from a brown leather case and began running the tip over the folds of fabric. She could hear something like static being emitted from the slightly bulbous tip.

"What's he doing?" she asked. She looked at the coffee table, where the brown tool case had been set without disturbing the magazines stacked there in neat piles. She could discern, on the unbuckled side clasp, an insignia of dense runic characters.

"This is a rather complicated operation," replied the supervisor, eyes fixed to his clipboard. "We've run partial tests, of course, but have never before attempted the complete sequence."

"Who do you work for?"

"We're longtime independent contractors," said the supervisor, looking up momentarily through spectacles that reflected her image back in wavering lines. "Because of the sensitivity of our projects, we are often brought in off the books."

"The Consortium?"

The supervisor hesitated, then nodded. "And other groups. Mainly in the private sector, though we have a growing presence in the public." He resumed taking notes. "This abbreviation has been in the planning for months."

"Abbreviation," she repeated. It was not a question. The word diffused and settled in the fissures between a host of discrete impressions, half-heard banalities, unspoken suspicions, revealing a topography as foreign as it was now coherent. She watched the supervisor continue to scribble; he had reached the last in a thick stack of forms. The tip of his pen seemed to cut deeply at the transparent clipboard, but when she glanced over his shoulder, she saw that the lines over which he so studiously labored were blank. A blast of cold came from behind. The sitting room window was opened. She saw two pairs of dress shoes on the fire escape; the heels seemed to elongate in ripples of air resembling the haze emitted from hot pavement.

The supervisor pocketed his pen and unclipped the finished packet. "Everyone desires progress," he said as he buckled his case. "Few acknowledge the practicalities of achieving it. Your efforts will not be forgotten. So to speak," he added, patting her lightly on the elbow. He stepped onto the windowsill. "Just remember—" His words were muffled by the sound of a plane skimming the rooftops. The windowsill was vacant. She watched a clump of feathers fall to the street below.

* * *

It occurred to her that she should shut the window, but her arms remained folded in front of her. The empty fire escape stood out with growing opacity in the slate gray dawn. Snow flurries rose and settled on the hardwood floor, but she felt nothing as she finally rose.

She took her time, struck by the branching of her customary path onto side streets dense with color. The streets grew crowded, but she was never rushed. She was early enough to see the muffin vendor still unpacking his things in front of her office building. She inserted her key card; the slot trundled its usual sequence allowing entry, followed by a long silence during which her card was not returned. The glass doors to the vestibule remained locked. She began her wait, a dimness in the glass against the reflections behind her.

Hopper emerged a little before six in the evening. He nodded at the security guard posted outside; the guard returned his nod without expression. She blocked his approach to a waiting taxi.

"When did you decide?" she asked.

"Does it really matter?" he replied. The guard looked over quizzically. Hopper took out his phone and dialed several digits, stopping one short of a phone number. He raised the receiver to his ear. "Hello? Yes, it's me," he said.

The waiting driver slapped one hand against the steering wheel and took off. "It's nothing new," Hopper was looking at her. "We're all parts of a life story. We just decided to find out how true that was."

"Am I the first?"

Hopper shook his head. The guard had resumed his impassive vigil. "But you are the most comprehensive. Even so, you're still considered a soft target. Few friends. No family. Of your own, that is."

"Did you know that before we met?"

"Some of it. The rest we figured out after." The dial pad on his phone began to flicker. He punched in another sequence of numbers.

She began to speak, but her words were absorbed in the growing wind.

He spoke into the receiver, but his eyes remained intently fixed on where she stood. "The last of it was this morning," he said.

"The last of what?" she asked. The wind picked up. She leaned into the gust and placed her hand over his. His knuckles were cold and sharp as he gripped the handle of his briefcase. The case shook slightly, then opened onto the pavement. The air was filled with shreds of paper. They twisted over Hopper's frantic hands. They skimmed the leaves of trees and settled thickly to the soil below. They traced vague shapes against the purple sky before assuming the translucence of flight.

Divination by Water

She nestled at the edge, enjoying the trickle and plash, the sensation of floating. The pool's gutter accommodated her perfectly. Every few moments, the overflow would wash warmly over her shoulders and outstretched arms. She bobbed her head to a melody she remembered hearing; when she attempted words to match the music, her face strained in concentration. She stopped after several tries, content to hum softly and watch her toenails waver like tiny corals in the currents below.

Water erupted at her side. A tall shape breached the surface, veiled in transparent tendrils. The only discernible feature was its mouth, stubbled and gasping. The mouth pursed around a large gulp of air. She watched its slow release through full lips. The mouth appraised her with a sliver of front teeth, weaving across dwindling ripples to join her. She watched its features coalesce, sharpen, and then blur again as it erased the intervening distance, attaching itself.

*   *   *

She broke away, laughing. She felt a pair of thumbs slide under the top of her bathing suit.

"Not here," she admonished.

"Who's going to see?" he asked, lowering his hands to her waist. He loosened his grip so she could lean around him. She leaned as far as she could but saw nothing beyond the rippling water and the dimly lit tiles on the other side.

"Where'd everybody go?" she asked.

"There's nobody else." He looked across the blue expanse. "The water's a lot warmer out there. C'mon."

"No!"

"I'll hold you up. I promise."

"I can't—" Her words were cut off by a long yawn. She sank neck deep and propped herself against the lip of the gutter.

*   *   *

"Hon?" he said.

"What?" She squinted at the wavering lines that scored the bottom of the pool.

"I was saying how nice this is. Just us."

"It hasn't been *that* long." Water dribbled into her eyes. She rubbed the sting out with one hand, careful to hold on with the other.

"Feels that way."

She turned. "What do you mean?"

He avoided her eyes and plunged under, rising again with a soft splash.

"What?" she repeated.

He shook his head and waded closer, gently grasping her by the hips. "I'm just glad to be here. With you."

She smiled. "Whatever."

"You want to finish this?" He held up a long flute, half full of frothy liquid that smelled like coconut.

She recoiled. "Ugh. I already feel hungover."

He drained the glass in a single swallow.

* * *

"Dance with me," she said.

"Here? In front of everybody?"

She rolled her eyes and paddled awkwardly toward him, hooking her arms around his neck. She pecked at his lips. She shivered slightly as his arms braced her.

He looked down at the inlet formed by their bodies. "I've never been very good at this," he said.

"Anyone can slow dance. All you need is a partner."

They drifted, turning slowly. She hummed the melody from before. At first, it had been clear and the words muddled, but now she was having trouble remembering the music as well. She hesitated.

"What's that?" he asked.

"Hmm?"

"That song."

She rested her cheek against his chest and shut her eyes. "You know. We were just listening to it."

"When?"

"Just now."

"We didn't bring any music."

"No music?" she said. "It's right—" She felt herself strain at his arms. His shoulders obscured the edges of the pool.

* * *

"It's getting late," she said.

"How can you tell?"

She stifled another yawn and then replaced her free hand on the dark blue gutter tiles. "What time is it?"

"I don't know," he answered.

She scanned the walls overhead. Except for the wavering light along a distant perimeter, their surroundings were dark.

"I don't think we're supposed to know."

She stared briefly. "You're acting weird. I'm going to bed." She began to lift herself out.

"You can't," he said. He was behind her now, knees squeezing her gently in place.

"Why not?" She let him hold her. Her hands swayed freely in the water.

"Because we're already in bed."

Her fingers stilled. "What did you say?"

"We're already in bed. Asleep."

She puffed her lips. "You're wasted," she said. She reached toward the edge of the pool.

"Wait," he said, pressing his lips to her ear.

"What are you—"

"Just listen."

"Stop . . . you're—"

"If we're really awake, how did we get here?"

She settled back onto his knees.

"Remember?"

She stared at the water overrunning the gutter's lip.

* * *

He began rocking her gently from side to side. "You don't remember because none of this is real."

"How?" she asked. "How can two people—"

"I read it somewhere."

"Where?"

"One of those papers. At the grocery store."

She craned her neck back and met his stare.

"Don't give me that look. I just believe in keeping an open mind."

She cupped some water in her hands and watched it dribble from the seam of her palms. "Two people. Same dream." She folded her arms and yielded to the sway of his body.

"Like they say about married people."

"We're not married," she said.

He stopped rocking and lowered them further into the water.

"Say it's true," she said.

"What?"

"This is all—"

"It *is* true."

"Your arms feel real. This water feels real."

"What about this?" he asked. She yelped at the pinch of his fingers on her hip. "Or this?" He pressed his lips to hers. His tongue worked at the seal of her mouth until she opened to receive him.

* * *

"Think about it. Why would we be here? Of all places."

She retreated along the edge. "You know I don't swim."

"Exactly."

"So?"

"I would never take you someplace you didn't want to go."

She let one arm move through the water. She pressed her cheek against the gutter's lip. The water rose level with her eyes, but she didn't blink. "What do you remember?"

"You couldn't sleep. We had just . . . you know."

She lifted her head and smiled.

"You wanted a glass of water. So I got out of bed. When I came back, you were out cold," he said.

"Then what?"

"Then I watched you sleep. I like watching you sleep."

She lifted her head up, tightening her grip on the edge.

"It's like I'm watching over you. Protecting you."

She nestled back against the pool's edge and poked her toes out of the water. "From what?"

"That movie star you're always talking about."

"I talk?"

"Kidding," he said. She slapped the surface of the water, splashing him.

* * *

He was kissing her neck just above the waterline.

"How do we wake up?"

"Don't you like it here?"

She leaned into him. "My dreams are never this quiet."

"Maybe it's a nightmare," he whispered into her shoulder.

"Stop."

"Like one of those shows. *When Sharks Go Apeshit*." He sank his teeth into her shoulder.

"Ow!"

"Sorry."

She pulled away. "You always do that," she said. "You're always—" She turned aside and started paddling away. "I'm getting out of here."

"Hon—"

"I want to wake up. Right now."

"Take it easy."

"Help me wake up. Help me—"

"It doesn't work like that."

"How do you know?"

He let himself drift away toward the center of the pool.

"Where are you going?" she asked.

"You figure it out."

She turned and studied her fingers. "Okay," she yelled over her shoulder. "I will." She propped herself up, using the gutter for support. Her arms shook from the effort and the cold on her wet skin. She sank back, shivering.

* * *

"I remember now," she said. "We were fighting."

"What?"

"We were fighting. Before."

He dove under and emerged inches from her perch at the edge.

"Before all this," she continued, "we were fighting. We were fighting, and I didn't want to. . . . So you got out of bed." She slid toward him. "You were gone a long time."

"I needed to—"

"That's not what I mean. I heard you open the medicine cabinet."
She slapped the water hard, sending spray into the air. "What were you
doing in the medicine cabinet?"

He shook himself off. "How could you even—"

"I've only asked you to oil the fucking door every day for the last
month."

He immersed himself up to his chin. "I had a headache. I took
something."

"I don't believe you."

"That was *your* excuse."

* * *

He floated toward her, making a show of how careful he was being,
paddling slowly so that only his head appeared above water. Despite
this, his approach caused icy wavelets to rise above the straps of her
bathing suit. She turned away and shivered into her folded arms.

"Hey," he said. He drifted behind her, lacing his fingers through
hers. He picked up a strand of hair clinging to her cheek and placed it
carefully behind her ear. She let him hold her.

"Don't you see how amazing this is? Our own little world. Nobody
else."

"That doesn't make any sense."

"What's sense got to do with anything? Here." He let go abruptly
and treaded water in front of her.

"What are you doing?"

"Close your eyes," he said.

"They're already closed."

"Good. Keep them that way."

She heard nothing beyond the slap of water against tiles.

"Just wait," he said. "I need to concentrate."

"What for?"

"I'm taking us somewhere else. Somewhere better. Watch. No—
wait. Eyes closed."

She heard a light splash nearby. "Where'd you go?" she asked.
"Where are you?"

"You did something."

He shook his head. "What did I do?"

"You did something to me."

"You think—"

She released the edge and flailed toward him. When she reached him, she grasped his waist and clambered up.

"I was mad," she said. "But—" She started coughing.

He raised her by the arms and propped her head on his shoulders. He stroked her back gently as it convulsed.

"You didn't have to . . ." she managed to whisper. "I say lots of things when I'm mad. We both do."

He swayed her from side to side until the coughing stopped. "You scared me."

"I'm sorry."

"You shouldn't scare me like that. Ever."

She had regained her breath, but the tightness of his grip made her breathing shallow. She could feel the shake of his shoulders at her chin. "Honey? Are you—"

"You shouldn't scare me like that," he repeated.

* * *

A grinning mass appeared, pink transparent plastic. Its thick tail, ridged like a dinosaur's, angled diagonally above the water. Its neck was long and segmented like a worm. The bulbous head was triangular, like its teeth, which were scrawled in an off-white patchwork along one side. The nostrils reminded her of a flaring horse's, while its eyes stared blankly at her, through the luster of beading water. Slowly, the float turned, revealing wings or arms that cleaved the water's surface. The neck, limbs, and tail were joined by a square base, with a hollow at the center the size of a child's torso. Water burbled along the edge of the hollow as the float completed its turn.

* * *

"I never dream about water," she said.

"Nobody remembers all their dreams."

"I remember enough." She spun around.

"This is different."

She slid herself over until she was directly in front of him. "You never answered me. What did you give me?"

"I swear—"

"We're not supposed to wake up. We're not supposed to. . . . This isn't—" She stopped and blinked. Water dripped from her cheeks and chin.

She tried to dodge his approach, but his arms were too quick. He linked his hands tightly over her belly and pulled her toward him.

"What did you do?"

"I needed to show you," he said.

"Show me what?"

He traced her earlobe with the tip of his nose. "Where you go, I go."

* * *

"I'm cold," she said.

He gripped her more tightly against him.

"I want to leave."

He kissed the line of her jaw. "We are."

"Tell me again."

"Tell you—"

"Tell me again."

He turned her around and held her head with both hands. "You have to trust me."

"I want . . . I want to leave."

"Then you know what we have to do."

She sobbed, pressing her eyes against his splayed thumbs. "Why?"

"Because it's the only way. Hey," he said, shaking her.

"I never—"

"Hey." He shook her more forcefully.

"Let go."

"Are you going to stop crying?"

She looked at him. His hands drifted to her sides.

"Ready?" he asked.

She nodded and settled herself next to him. She pressed her feet to the tiles. She looked for her ankles in the churn of sudden current. She bent with him as he leaned back.

"Will you make me breakfast?" she asked.

His grip on her slackened. "What?"

"In the morning. Will you make me breakfast?"

"Sure." She could see his teeth smile in the periphery of her vision. She readied herself, knees just breaching the surface.

"I'm not cold anymore."

"No?"

"The water feels soft. Like—"

"Blankets?"

She nodded. "Blankets. And blue. It's like—" Her breath caught. The water was up to her chin now.

"Don't," he said. He gripped her shoulder.

They leaned once more toward the tiles, which reflected them back in concentric streaks. Together they pushed off.

Nuptial Superstitions of the West

Old

If one were to believe the preponderance of paranormal encounter narratives, one would likely live in fear of—or hope for—the plethora of strange detours afforded by ordinary circumstances. Ghosts haunt offices and rural roadsides; aliens hunt abductees in supermarket parking lots; spouses vanish from cornfields, birthday parties, honeymoons, cars in midcommute. Enter an elevator at a certain hour of night—for the paranormalist, your chances of perishing from mechanical failure are exponentially outweighed by the likelihood that you will emerge far in space and time from your intended floor.

The same cannot be said of weddings. Any number of paranormal events may *surround* a wedding. A proposal's acceptance coincides with the flight of doves from nearby shrubbery. The rain expected to dampen a nuptial weekend clears brilliantly just before the ceremony. Or, as in the recent reception staple "Save a Dance for Daddy" by country musician Bo Lovell, a grizzled Gulf War veteran returns to attend his daughter's wedding; by the last verse, we learn he has been killed in action and is attending the ceremony literally in spirit before "dancing to my Great Reward." But the spirits hold their peace, yeti and Sasquatch admit no impediment, the fabric of the cosmos is not torn asunder.

Recently, I spent most of an afternoon in the stacks of the public library's central branch, looking for stories of the unexplained at weddings or wedding receptions. Even with the latter expanded search terms, I failed to find a single documented narrative or eyewitness account. Several hours into my search, I cheered triumphantly—to the annoyance of a transient pair dozing drunkenly nearby—as the computer returned a reference to Helen Tremaine's *Wedding Disasters*. I should have suspected a false lead from the title's listing under customs, etiquette, and folklore. I was perhaps overly eager from so much time spent fruitlessly. Not until I had the volume in my hands did I read its full title: *Wedding Disasters and How to Avoid Them: How to Plan (and Enjoy!) Your Special Day.* I perused the table of contents on the chance that the author included a relevant chapter, or at least an anecdote or two. Apart from dismissing the recent fashion for throwing birdseed at departing newlyweds (the deadliness of rice was pure urban legend) and encouraging the bride to put her own stamp on wedding tradition ("Every bride needs something old, something new, something borrowed, and everything fabulous!"), the disasters were all hypothetical, easily thwarted by the proper application of platitude and exclamation point. The lights overhead began blinking on and off, a signal that the library was about to close. I proceeded to the exit.

There are, of course, less trivial impediments to the marriage of true minds. The recent indictment of a Michigan groom for allegedly leaving his bride to drown during their Australian honeymoon; the abandonment at the altar of a New York City bride who, at the reception, now held to celebrate singlehood regained, shuffled bravely to the defiant strains of Gloria Gaynor; the well-documented story of the groom who toasted his guests with compromising photographs of the bride and best man left beneath every chair in the reception hall—these and countless other nuptial misfortunes seem to justify the smug proprieties that accompany the successful exchange of vows. But the motives behind such derelictions are easily attributed. There is nothing of the supernatural in a partner's greed or infidelity. Nature has proven itself to be largely polygamous; we are one of the few species to practice monogamy and the only one, as far as we know, of sufficient intelligence—or lack thereof—to ordain with ceremony our biological imperative to reproduce.

The best-known—albeit fictional—paranormal wedding narrative must certainly be Coleridge's "The Rime of the Ancient Mariner," though the wedding is more of a framing device for the mariner's tale of avenging spirits and monsters at sea:

> It is an ancient mariner
> And he stoppeth one of three.
> "By thy long grey beard and glittering eye,
> Now wherefore stoppest thou me?
>
> The bridegroom's doors are opened wide,
> And I am next of kin;
> The guests are met, the feast is set:
> Mayst hear the merry din."
>
> [The mariner] holds him with his skinny hand,
> "There was a ship," quoth he.

Of more recent provenance is the tale of a wedding guest who, to lighten the mood of the long reception line, decided to share a quaint and only slightly risqué bit of wedding night wisdom with the bride and groom. Having embraced the newlyweds, he withdrew slightly, keeping one hand on each of their adjacent shoulders.

"Well," he began, in the deadpan he had practiced carefully the day before in the rental car from the airport, "hope you guys don't wear each other out tonight."

Had he been less intent on his engaging punch line, he would have noticed the matron next in line swivel her head abruptly in his direction.

The groom, whose practiced smile wavered slightly, patted the guest warmly on the back, perhaps to dissemble his complete lack of recognition. "Thanks, guy," he said, cocking one hand like a pistol and winking suggestively.

The guest, anxious that his remarks would lose their humorous effect if broken up by the groom's glib riposte, began again. "Seriously. You guys should really take it easy on each other—"

The bride interrupted, grinning stiffly. "We're *so* glad you could make it," she said. She indicated the matron with the slightest shake of her head. "I don't know if you know my *grandmother*, who flew all the way from *Albuquerque*."

The guest offered the grandmother his hand; the grandmother shook it limply, her expression cool. The punch line would have to stand on its own.

"Anyway—" In mid-sentence, he felt the groom begin to guide him onward. Before he was out of earshot, the guest hurriedly elaborated on the folkloric context of his perhaps off-color but nevertheless well-intentioned remarks: the superstitious belief that the first to fall asleep on the wedding bed will be the first to die. "So, you know, try not to kill each other tonight." He chuckled to signal his humorous intent, clasping the groom's shoulder. The grandmother stepped into the narrow space between them and silenced the guest with a discreet elbow to the ribs. She veiled the blow with vociferous praise of the ceremony and the bride's gown. Rather than embarrass her by reacting—the gauntness of her arm sharpened the impact considerably—the guest moved aside without protest to accommodate her ill-gotten audience.

The lingering guest now dispatched, the line moved briskly. The bride and groom endured the fraught permutations of wedding portraiture with relatively little fuss (the bride's estranged older brother hesitated briefly before posing with the wedding party; her mother-in-law demanded the same position in every shot to guarantee posterity her most flattering side). The reception was sufficiently lavish, despite the lack of a pork entrée and a minor malfunction in the third tier of the champagne fountain. Despite loving threats before the ceremony—and the goading of several drunken guests—the feeding of the cake left neither newlywed unpleasantly smeared. The garter and bouquet toss produced a happy pairing, if not from this day forward, at least for part of the night. At eleven, the bride and groom retreated discreetly to the nearest elevator to the honeymoon suite. Despite their exhaustion, they mustered more than enough energy to consecrate their union beneath a canopy of seafoam stripes. They fed each other strawberries and squares of chocolate from the gift basket provided compliments of the hotel. They extinguished their bedside lamps and spooned in the breeze from their open balcony, talking softly in the dark.

As the light over the Pacific went from black to deep indigo, they had yet to fall asleep.

The groom sat up and padded to the bathroom. The bride hit the lights on her side of the bed. Her husband squinted over a tumbler of water. He took several sips and passed the glass to the bride.

"I'm still so wired," said the groom, stretching his arms toward the ceiling. He propped up several pillows and leaned back against them. "Still coming down, I guess. From everything."

The bride said nothing as she drank.

"You'd think we'd both be exhausted. We've been up for—" He looked at the red digits of the sleek black clock glowing against the mahogany nightstand. "Hours," he continued. "But here we are. Both of us. Wide awake."

Still the bride said nothing. She drained the glass and set it down next to her side of the bed. She reached for the phone.

The groom looked over, confused. "I think it's too late for room service."

The bride continued dialing. "I'm not calling room service."

Five floors down, the phone in my room started ringing.

New

The ancient Greeks considered balance to be divine and calculated its exact numerical proportions, replicating them in the dimensions of their temples and statuary. During the Renaissance, balance was a matter of perspective, allowing the flat canvas to assume the fullness of three dimensions. Asymmetry, by contrast, provokes and disturbs. The photographer crops unevenly to create expectation of what is outside the frame; the off-center shot in film foreshadows trouble. Our predilection for balance extends as far back as the occult origins of civilization. In numerology, the number two represents unity and completion. The number one stands for ambition and drive, but it is also associated with restlessness and the persistence of desire unfulfilled. To refer to one's "better half" is thus more than affectionate flattery—it is the expression of an archetypal impulse, as old as the caveman's mute foreboding as he stared skyward into the jagged tusk of a waning moon.

The women at my table acknowledged these remarks with polite indifference. I will not detain the reader with a catalog of excuses for my unsolicited disquisition, although these were certainly in abundance: the late arrival of my flight the night before after several delays; the cocktails I had consumed earlier on an empty stomach; the wine I subsequently consumed to accompany my chicken cordon bleu and mixed seasonal greens; my self-consciousness as I introduced myself to the woman sitting next to me; my disappointment on seeing her ring finger, where the snout of a diamond perched in reproach; my neighbor's far less attractive friend, who asked for every detail of the impending nuptials, swooning with anticipatory relish that barely disguised her seething envy. "You're *so* his better half," she said, prompting protest from the bride-to-be. "I mean it. You're like the person that completes him. You know? Like in that movie—" Here is where I interrupted, less to be helpful than to relieve the beginnings of a hangover.

Before continuing, I would like to make one thing clear: I am not the sort of person who resents love. Indeed, I celebrate love. I admire the serendipity that brings two people together, the persistence that keeps them together over time or distance or both, the commitment they share on occasions just like this. Yet would one choose to feast on such rich food every day? We savor turkey and ham on holidays, the sweetness of birthday cake. But their richness is enhanced because of their rarity, whereas a daily diet of them would quickly dull our palates. And so I enjoy the occasional romance matinee. I welcome calls from friends, breathless with news of their latest flirtations or more serious prospects, only screening when prior commitments prevent my focused attention. I am no less avid than the rest of my dinner companions when, between courses, a couple dissects with forensic precision the exact circumstances (the sunlit curls *that stopped me in my tracks*; the virile baritone *that turned my knees to jelly*) to which we owe their felicitous pairing. It is to appreciate moments such as these as fully as possible that, for much of the year, I studiously avoid the least possibility of encountering them.

Nevertheless, when the bride invited me, I felt obliged to go. We've known each other since college and, for several years after graduation, we lived in the same city. We would see each other frequently, as her office was only two blocks from Déjà Lu, the used bookstore where I served as cashier and was recently promoted to assistant manager. Despite regular gatherings for drinks or dinner, we lost touch, apart from the occasional card or e-mail, after she was moved to her company's western headquarters. There, she met the groom, then a medical student, now a resident in internal medicine at one of the nation's premier teaching hospitals. I first met the groom at the rehearsal dinner the night before; he seemed perfectly affable despite being primarily conversant in ESPN's *SportsCenter*.

The soundtrack for dessert was Anthony Bristow. I was struck by the odd coincidence as he had lately become an important addition to Déjà Lu's growing music department. Among my newly assumed responsibilities was the whiteboard above the cash register. Here, management recommended recently arrived used records. The board was split down the middle by a red line of dry-erase ink. On the left side— IF YOU ARE—the store listed a timely selection of customers' possible moods or states of mind: IF YOU ARE / OFF TO THE BEACH / SEXLESS IN THE CITY / AFRAID FOR YOUR DWINDLING CIVIL LIBERTIES. On the right side—YOU MIGHT ENJOY—were the store's corresponding recommendations: VAMPIRE WEEKEND / GOLDFRAPP / VOTING NEXT TIME. After hearing most of the singer's new record in line at the local deli, I was moved to add to the whiteboard after lunch: IF YOU ARE / DEAD INSIDE / YOU MIGHT ENJOY / ANTHONY BRISTOW.

The chatter at my table resumed. The bride-to-be's friend dabbed with her fork at a sliver of tiramisu. "Oh, I *love* this song. Don't you love this song?" She turned to the rest of the table, mostly friends of the groom from medical school who had vacated their seats for the bar. "Do you know what your song's gonna be?" she asked.

The bride-to-be shook her head. "We haven't decided yet. I sort of want that song I told you about. Remember? The one that goes—" Here she affected the soft warble of Nellie McKay.

"She's being ironic," I said.

Her eyes narrowed. "Who is?" she asked.

"That singer. About getting married. She's not being serious."

Her friend leaned over a shallow pool of sugary mush. "Do you know what *you're* being right now?"

"I'm just saying," I retorted. "People only hear the melody. No one ever listens to the words."

"Well, right now, none of us wants to listen to you." She raised a hand parallel to the side of her face, a fashionable gesture denoting the end of her receptivity.

I felt a tap at my shoulder. I was relieved to see the bride leaning into my periphery. "Why aren't you dancing?" she asked. I said nothing and drained my wine glass. She extended her hand resolutely. "You know it's bad luck not to dance with the bride if she asks."

"Bad luck for who?" I asked.

Her hand flattened with insistence. "C'mon," she said.

I allowed myself to be led to the floor, where several couples twirled in loose clusters to Frank Sinatra. I felt my feet drag heavily next to her heels, but after a few measures, we were swaying easily in time.

"Is there anyone else here I can offend?" I asked. "I think I'm done with most of your coworkers."

She laughed over my shoulder. "I told Grammy you have Tourette's."

"You didn't."

She nodded. I looked down at my feet again.

"Are you having a good time?" she asked.

"Sure," I said. "It beats drinks at Ike's."

"Ugh . . . you still go there?"

"Not with the rent I'm paying." Sinatra's voice swelled to fill a brief silence. "You shouldn't worry about me," I said. "I'm fine."

"You read about—"

"It's the *New York Times*. It gets around."

The bride looked up toward the surrounding tables. "She has great timing, as always."

"It doesn't matter."

"You didn't have to come. I would have understood." I looked at her. "I wanted to be here. Really."

"What's it been?"

"A few years." Her eyes remained locked on mine. "Give or take a few more years."

"This couldn't have been a surprise. I mean—"

"Of course not. Did you know in a recent study of bats, almost ninety percent of females preferred gainfully employed male bats with thinning hair and bad skin?"

A bridesmaid approached and whispered in the bride's ear. "I have to go," the bride said. "Try and have a good time? Not for me—for you?" She vanished into the gathering crowd clumping in pairs to Al Green.

* * *

If my single tablemate took offense at dinner, all was forgiven by the bouquet toss. She emerged from a flurry of outstretched hands bearing the prize clenched tightly to her chest. She leaped repeatedly in triumph before being gently escorted back to her table. I congratulated her as she walked past in a cloud of pungent perfume.

At the front of the ballroom, the DJ leaned into his microphone. "The fun's not over yet, ladies and gentlemen. It's the guys' turn now. I need all the single men in the room to report to the dance floor immediately." The seated bride and standing groom were already there. I stared at the slick tumbler in my hand, unsure of where it had come from. The bride rose slightly from her chair and scanned the room. I shrugged, the glass now empty, and stood. I was halfway across the floor when I noticed the only other single making his way to the front. I slowed my steps, looking for the nearest exit. I stared into a solid wall of pumps, wing tips, and sandals. "C'mon, fellas. Don't be shy. There's nothing wrong with being a loser—I mean ladies' man." There was scattered booing and applause. "C'mon, guys. Hurry it up. The groom's hoping to get lucky tonight."

The DJ put on a burlesque melody and proceeded to give instructions. The bride hiked her skirts while the groom kneeled. ("Looks like this one knows his way around down there!") He reached up and pulled the garter off her leg. "Now you guys," the DJ said, pointing at us, "take a few steps back . . . back . . . more . . . that's it, keep going. . . . We don't want to make it too easy." We were at the dance floor's midpoint by the time he told us to stop. The groom's back was a rippling silhouette in the distance next to the blur of the bride's dress. I felt my knees begin to buckle as the DJ counted. "On three. . . . One . . . two . . . three!" There was a drumroll. The garter disappeared into the lights overhead. I waited, almost forgetting to raise my arms. I could only guess the garter's trajectory as I stared into the glare of chandeliers. There was cheering all of a sudden; I clenched my empty fingers with relief. I began to bolt back to my seat when I noticed the loop of lace dangling from my chest. The garter was suspended from my tie tack. It was fixed there so firmly that removing it caused the material to tear slightly.

"Easy there, cowboy," said the DJ, winking. "Getting it off's only half the fun." The bride had vacated her seat; the chair was now occupied by the girl with the bouquet. A few petals tumbled from her lap to the floor. She had removed her shoes; her toenails looked coppery stubbed beneath her stockings.

"OK," the DJ continued, "now this next part is crucial. You paying attention? Or are you too busy trying to look up the pretty lady's skirt? . . . Your mission, should you choose to accept it"—I will let the reader fill in the most appropriate musical accompaniment—"is to slide that garter up the lady's leg as far as it will go. The higher you go, the better luck for the bride and groom."

I was, needless to say, rather skeptical about the provenance of this superstition—it had no precedent in the texts I could recall offhand—but the music was too loud for me to make my queries heard, much less understood. I went down on one knee. The blare of brass was soon joined by whistling and more applause. Her foot slid between my palms. Her big toe dug sharply at my wrist. I looked up and caught her wink.

I proceeded to honor the bride and groom. It did not occur to me to consult with my presumptive partner about the extent of my reach. The clapping grew louder, more rhythmic as I eased the lace further up. Her mouth, rimmed with sweat, smiled tautly. Somewhere above the knee, her thighs squeezed my fingers to a stop. I sank into the warm pressure. She yielded another inch, then another. Finally, I stopped. I gave her thigh a firm pinch as I withdrew. Her yelp of surprise was masked by the music in front of us and the shrillness behind.

"Let's give these two some room," said the DJ, introducing Marvin Gaye. We were clenched together now at the waist.

I felt her mouth at my ear. "You're bad," she said, with a trace of admonition, but I could feel her stomach flutter through her dress. She lowered her voice to a whisper. "Did you like that?" I nodded wordlessly. She leaned against my shoulder, facing out. Others had joined us but swayed along at a discreet remove. Her lips grazed my ear again. "I think you're cute," she said. "As long as you keep your mouth shut." She laughed and leaned back onto my shoulder. "Why is that, anyway?"

"Why's what?"

"Guys are so weird. They treat you like shit in front of everybody. But get them alone and they can't keep their hands to themselves."

"Is that what they do with you?"

She looked away for a second before answering. "Sometimes." She leaned in again.

"I couldn't help myself," I said.

"Really?"

"Mmhmm."

She smiled. Her hands hung damply at the back of my neck. "And what made me so irresistible?"

"You really want to know?"

She nodded, her lips parted slightly.

"Alcohol, mostly," I said. "Alcohol and desperation."

Her mouth flattened to a pallid line. She pulled away.

"I'm sorry," I said. "Come back." But the laughter kept rising from my throat. I laughed as I watched the back of her dress retreat between stilled dancers. I laughed through Marvin Gaye and half of "Love Shack." I laughed until my eyes stung, streaking the sides of my face.

The Devil and the Dairy Princess

* * *

The singer Graham Parker once compared the hangover—specifi-
cally, the din that seems to line the skull the morning after overindulg-
ing—to canned laughter. I can personally attest to the accuracy of this
description. Canned laughter certainly goes a long way toward captur-
ing its essence, but there are certain layers and nuances that escape
the concision of popular song—much as I admire the latter form and
Parker's work in particular. There is, for example, the further echo of
voices raised across the whole spectrum of human emotion: curiosity,
disbelief, indignant seething, simmering animosity, full-blown rage.
There is the sense memory of your own cloudy actions and reactions:
the tightness in your throat as you raised your own voice (in defense?
in song?); the clutch of objects that were not yours for the taking (another's drink? the DJ's microphone?). There is the impression of halting
conversation with disinterested silhouettes in tuxedo jackets and pas-
tels. Perhaps you have not been heard, so you talk louder into the din.
The music cuts off. You are shouting into a pillow, alone under sweaty
sheets.

To these impressions may be added the chirp of the phone on one's
nightstand.

"Hello?" I croaked into the receiver.

"Get up here. Now." The voice gave a room number before abruptly
hanging up. I stared feverishly into the darkness as I placed the source
of the call.

The bride was summoning me.

* * *

The hotel's air-conditioned corridor was a relief from the damp
swaddling in which I'd woken up. Except for my blazer, which was nowhere to be found, I was still dressed—shoes and all—so after some
initial confusion, it took only a few moments to get to the elevators. But
as soon as the doors closed and the car began its ascent, I felt a burning
knot rising rapidly to my throat. I swallowed hard. The elevator stopped.

The door to the honeymoon suite was already open. I knocked
anyway. The groom answered in a dark blue terry cloth robe and led me

toward a seat facing the bed. I was distracted from my nausea by the wide dimensions of the room.

Before I could ask about the bride, she emerged from the bathroom carrying a glass of water. She wore a robe matching the groom's. She didn't look at me as she joined us.

"If this is about the reception, I think I've apologized. Multiple times."

The bride gave me a look that instantly silenced me. "You're not here because of that," she said. She briefly noticed my dishevelment. "You want some water?"

I swallowed again and felt my stomach settle tenuously. "I'm fine."

"I'm glad," said the bride. "I'm glad you're fine. We"—here she glanced at the groom—"were just talking about you."

"You were?"

The bride nodded. "Among other things. Sports. Current events."

"Those are really the same thing, you know."

"Shut up," the bride said. The groom raised one hand in a calming gesture. "We've been up here. Together. On our wedding night. The happiest day of our lives."

"So far," added the groom.

"So far," acknowledged the bride. "We've had a beautiful day. The usual last-minute stuff with flowers and catering. But otherwise, it's gone as well as anyone would want." She joined hands with the groom. "I . . . *we* are happy. We've had a beautiful day. And a beautiful night."

The groom grinned, mildly embarrassed, before speaking. "Only thing is—"

"You can't sleep," I said, remembering the reception line. "You can't—" I laughed, each chuckle sending a sharp throb to the center of my forehead. I closed my eyes and waited for the pounding to stop. When I opened them, the bride was watching me.

"Oh, come on," I said. "You have to admit, this is sort of funny."

The bride gestured for me to be quiet. "I know it is. But he—" The groom opened his mouth as if to interrupt. "*We* just thought since we were up—"

"—you could tell us more," said the groom. "Like maybe there's something we could do to break the spell."

"Spell? What spell?" The throb resumed as I sat up. "You know what they say about superstitions."

"What?" asked the groom, eagerly.

"They're only true if you believe them."

The bride took a seat on the edge of the bed next to the groom, looking down at the plush carpet.

The groom put an arm around her. "If the Soporex doesn't work, I've got something stronger—"

"I knew it," she said, brushing him away. "Things were just going too well...." Her voice caught but she quickly regained her composure. She looked up. "You're right, though. It is sort of funny. As wedding disasters go."

"No," I said. "Don't say that. What I said before, forget it. It's bullshit."

The groom stood up hopefully. "You made it up?"

"Not all of it.... But that's not important. The important thing is that you're together. Who cares who falls asleep first? You have years with each other." I tried to rest a consoling hand on the bride's arm, but she stood and went to the suite's wide windows. The curtains were open; the harbor outside was now visible in the graying light.

"You know I used to have a thing for you," she said.

The groom and I looked at each other.

"This was a long time ago. Long before I met him." She took a seat on a nearby wing chair. She crossed her bare legs, swinging one over the other as she spoke. "Remember that summer I was living around Eastern Market?"

"Yeah."

"My roommate was out of town on the Fourth. We were meeting everybody at the Mall. I wore that blue seersucker dress, with the straps? The one you liked on me."

I looked at the groom. "I never—"

"Oh, you liked it," she said. "I didn't really have it planned out. I would just wait until the right moment. You know, maybe during the fireworks. But that would be sort of cheesy. Maybe after, with all the smoke. We could just sneak off somewhere."

I could taste the return of my nausea. "I—I had no idea."

"Of course you didn't." She turned to her husband. "I was giving him every possible sign. Laughing hysterically at everything he said. And you know he's not that funny."

"I've got the picture," said the groom.

"And all he can talk about—before, during, and after—was Denise, Denise, Denise. Denise still hasn't returned my phone call. Denise returned my phone call, but she sounded weird. Denise forgot our ten-week anniversary."

"Twelve weeks," I said. "It was twelve—"

"She was two time zones away. What did you expect? Anyway, you did me a favor. When I stopped feeling sorry for you, I stopped feeling anything at all." She stood and rejoined her husband on the bed. "He's right," she told him. "We're fine. We're going to be fine. Because this is real."

"That's not fair," I said. "She's still—"

"Fucking someone else. Married to someone else. Having someone else's babies. For your sake, there better be an afterlife. That's the only future in loving a ghost."

I stood. The room was spinning now. I prepared to run to the bathroom, but all that came out was a burning belch.

"You OK?" asked the groom. "Let me get you some water." When I started slumping again, he guided me gently to the bed. The bride was at the window, steeped in the growing light from the harbor.

The groom returned with a full glass. I could think of nothing to say as I drank.

After several minutes, the groom cleared his throat. "You know, maybe we're thinking about this all wrong. This is really just a good excuse to keep the party going."

"Honey, no." The bride turned from the window. She seemed more relaxed, but her eyes avoided mine as she left the area of the balcony. "I'm so tired—"

"Well then, why don't you go to sleep?" he said. They exchanged a brief look. He began working the dial of a portable music player. "Most of this is mood music for us, but we must have burned something you like. What're you in the mood for?" he asked as he fixed the player into the bedside speaker dock.

"Whatever," I said. I pressed the cold glass to my forehead and closed my eyes.

"Here you go. *The Very Best of Elvis Costello and the Attractions.* You're into that New Wave stuff, right?"

I opened my eyes. "That collection is for dilettantes. It barely scratches the surface." I was about to go into the glaring discographic omissions when I noticed the bride's brittle glare. "That would be perfect. Thank you," I said.

We listened to "Alison" and then "Watching the Detectives." The opening drums on "Chelsea" felt like they were being played against my temples. The groom refilled my glass and filled one of his own. I took a few sips, but mostly I just liked the coolness of the wet glass on my forehead.

The groom stood over me. "How're you feeling? Better?" he asked.

I nodded.

"Anything else I can get for you?"

"No," I said, then noticed the blurred outline of the groom through the glass. The bubbles along the sides looked soapy. And some held their shape as they sunk to the bottom in opaque shards.

I set the glass somewhere on my lap. Both newlyweds were in front of me now, watching. I felt myself sink back under the nuptial canopy. Words were suddenly hard to remember, but I managed to make myself understood.

"Was all that true?" I asked. "That time on the Mall?"

"You know what they say about superstitions," said the bride. She snatched the glass from my hand before it tipped onto the carpet. My eyes shut.

Borrowed

"I fear thee, ancient mariner!
I fear thy skinny hand!
And thou art long, and lank, and brown,
As is the ribbed sea-sand.

I fear thee and thy glittering eye,
And thy skinny hand, so brown."

Blue

I heard, before I could see, a humming echo that seemed to carry me upward to breach. The surface was solid black but then lightened to blue. I could make out the ripple of currents overhead. In their approaching transparency, I could see clouds and the outlines of sea birds. I rose faster, bracing for the shock of breath.

The bridal suite was fully lit in the overcast late morning. The music had looped back to the long fade-out of "Accidents Will Happen." By the curtains parted over the harbor, the newlyweds dozed together upright on a chair, each tilted over an armrest, heads lolling awkwardly over the narrow space between.

I left and took the elevator down to the lobby. Outside, I crossed the parking lot and the adjoining street to the rocks at the harbor's edge. The higher rocks were sandy and dry, but the lower I went, the more fresh seaweed rose and fell with the current. In the pools along the water's surface, black crabs gathered, alternately submerged and scrambling along the stones left glistening by the retreating tide. They scrabbled over the tips of my shoes; the leather was too smooth for their claws to find traction. The tide returned, higher this time. I watched my feet sink into a pool festooned with kelp. The water had an inviting warmth—only when the tide retreated did I feel the clammy heaviness of my legs. The next wave sprayed foam above my knees and pulled at the cuffs of my pants. I waited. The sea in folklore is charmed, rising to take you to other worlds that, only in the guise of this one, could be mistaken for oblivion. But my head was clear, and my feet were cold, and my stomach churned with appetite. I clambered back, in search of breakfast.

The Devil and the Dairy Princess

The Possession of
Charles Ignatius de Leon

Charles Ignatius de Leon was laid to rest with the spectacle and bene-
diction just shy of those reserved for high-ranking clergy. The Pope
himself sent condolences to his native parish; his casket was borne by
three generations of Knights of Columbus, who were proud to consider
themselves sons of the childless departed. He joined his wife Georgina
in the shade of ancient lindens overhanging a modest plot, two blocks
west of Christ the Redeemer, where they were married nearly thirty-
seven years to the day.

Beyond the province of the city's independent living community,
de Leon was a fixture as a pundit on radio and television. He was president of the local League of Family Voters, a watchdog group that, at

the time of de Leon's fatal coronary, boasted upward of 200,000 dues-paying members nationwide; an outpost overlooking K Street in Washington, DC; and millions perusing the online edition of *Hestia*, the League's quarterly clearinghouse of opinion and legislative developments at both state and federal levels. An unabashed freethinker—only the lockstep Left would brand him a conservative—de Leon relished the opportunity to debate the League's expansive platform. "Debate" was a generous word to reluctant but determined opponents; he was known as "El Chillón" ("The Loudmouth") by immigrant rights advocates for his shrill defense of our weakening borders. He was equally adept at combating uninformed attacks on religious freedom, intelligent design, national security, and sexual reeducation. As Chuck de Leon ("King of the Talk Jungle"), he hosted a popular syndicated radio program. His sizeable donation toward the renovation of St. Agatha's on the occasion of his sixty years as a baptized Catholic was rejected after protest by numerous parishioners; the funds were subsequently accepted without comment by a representative of the diocese. His full-page ads in regional newspapers and magazines—augmented by devil horns and Hitler mustaches—were popular decorations at parties mourning electoral results in 2000 and 2004.

* * *

Carlos Ignacio de Leon was born on a scalding August evening in 1938 on the outskirts of Milford, California. The alias he would assume for most of his adult life was motivated by pride and fear, which, for the freshly minted patriot, are never mutually exclusive. De Leon is an abbreviation of a longer surname now lost to us, the shorter version deemed more acceptably European by the boy's paternal grandparents. His choice of cognates was his own; he soon grew tired of the violence done to his given names by the American tongue. Patiently, he would feed himself like spare change into the coin slot of an interlocutor's attention, only to be dispensed any number of garish novelties: Juan, Raúl, José, Pablo. Whether his parents disapproved of abandoning treasured family nomenclature—a beloved uncle's middle name, the patron saint of his grandparents' birthplace—is unclear from the available record.

The Devil and the Dairy Princess

His father, the area's most trusted grocer, was a practical man who recognized in his son the makings of an impractical adult. Nevertheless, he was patient as the boy helped to sift apples into bins and stocked shelves with fresh bread and pastries. His mother, sometime baker and seamstress for her husband's franchise, was more suspicious. Charles displayed an early predilection for drawing and sculpture, shaping birds and fish out of wood salvaged from broken crates. Doña de Leon, who nearly accepted the proposal of an itinerant painter before persuading herself that the contingencies of art were best suffered alone, frowned over these first fruits of obvious talent. She assented to their sale as toys and Christmas ornaments but hoarded the proceeds for liturgical necessities: candles for the family's shrine to the saints, Easter lilies, a new shirt for her son's First Communion. In the de Leon household, everything was assigned a ledger in which balance was scrupulously maintained.

Nevertheless, as an only child, he was doted on by both parents. The forward-thinking de Leons never resorted to corporal punishment as discipline; they had learned well from their agrarian patrons that the broader the pasture, the less room to stray. If there was ever the temptation to apply more traditional goads, Charles was too far away for it to matter. A quiet yet precocious student, he had earned a full scholarship to agriculture school but quickly lost interest in the science of crops and livestock. The sole appeal of the clustered bungalows and scrub of the modest campus was the surrounding landscape, which the frustrated artist found inspiring. He skipped laboratory sessions and exams with greater frequency to borrow a car and wander the eucalyptus and oak groves trafficked by coyotes, burrowing owls, and the occasional interstate truck.

One of his excursions took him to a clearing of boulders whose symmetrical arrangement suggested handiwork too precise to be nature's alone. He exited the car on arriving, yawned and stretched. As soon as he heard the car door shut behind him, he felt the lightness of his pockets and cursed. In his eagerness, he had forgotten the money set aside to fuel his return trip. With the acumen inherited from his parents and the restraint of the starving student, he had calculated to the penny the exact amount he would need to fuel his drive back to campus. For all he knew, the money he had so carefully set aside was being used by his roommate to treat local girls of questionable age at the local bar. Dreading the long walk ahead, he entered the clearing and made his way to the rock formation a quarter of a mile away.

The boy had grown up with all sorts of legends about the land surrounding Milford, stories of delicate flints buried further down than any arrowhead, and trace settlements of ancestry long preceding the oldest living natives. As he approached the triangular structure, he felt years of forgotten lore return all at once in the silence that swallowed his footfalls. The lone triangle turned out to be a triad—one larger flanked by two proportionally smaller ones set in the foreground. Seen straight on, the grouping appeared as one solid shape; only when near enough could de Leon discern the narrow space demarcated by the smaller triangles in front. He entered this space now with a reverence he had never felt in church. He kneeled before the larger boulder and studied the wall it formed before him. Petroglyphs were etched in the rock, alternately resembling alien script and the most intricate pictorial shapes. He studied them closely, withdrawing his sketch pad to record their textures under the shifting light. He worked until the light completely failed him. Exhausted, he collapsed to the coppery earth and slept impassively until morning. He arose refreshed despite the austerity of his pallet. A further omen awaited him in the abandoned car. Rifling hopefully through his satchel for the makings of breakfast, his eyes were drawn to the ruffled floor mat. Through a crust of dirt, he could clearly discern the outline of several coins.

He returned to campus in time for a late-morning chemistry lecture, which he skipped the better to expedite news of his decision to quit school. Half of Milford was privy to his parents' outrage; the call came at a particularly busy time following the arrival of fresh produce. His mother was content to express her grief sobbing inarticulately at her husband's side. The proprietor himself, as if making up for years of withholding pronouncement of the obvious, exhausted the invective of both his native languages to berate his son. He had nothing against art—here he braced himself out of habit, but Doña de Leon's disapproving glare was not forthcoming—only the artist's lifestyle. He felt betrayed; to have worked and saved to afford a life of comfort, free of any want, for his only child and then have that legacy shrugged off—voluntarily, he stressed, acid edging every syllable—as if discarding rags unfit even for the beggar his son would no doubt become—

Carlos Ignacio blanched at the sound of his given name spit from his father's mouth. But he waited out the torrent to illuminate the signposts of his chosen path: There was a new language being spoken in the ravings of Ivy League expatriates, coursing from the horns and keys of shamanic musicians. Entire lives were being lived on the road, pledged to the poetry of drifting.

"On the road?" his father asked. "On the road?" His rage by now had ebbed, depleted to non sequiturs. "How do they go to the bathroom?"

His son hung up the receiver.

* * *

While a complete itinerary is impossible, fragmentary evidence suggests that the artist spent the entirety of his early career in the American West. An unlabeled folder in de Leon's archive contained a number of leaflets advertising group exhibitions featuring his work in Seattle, San Francisco, Oakland, and Albuquerque. Also recovered was the bound catalog of a solo show held in the fall of 1964 at the Clay Dennis Gallery near San Jose. The catalog featured several reproductions of landscapes, self-portraits, and what appear to be figure studies, as well as a photograph that appears to show the artist working in his studio. The de Leon estate subsequently requested the entire contents of the folder for inspection and documentation. These materials have since been lost.

* * *

One can only speculate what brought him to the tiny desert town of Recursos, New Mexico. His arrival would have been impossible except by car, suggesting that his prospects as a working artist may not have been as dire as his parents predicted. This would have been decades before the town's ascendancy as an enclave for writers, painters, and people of conscience driven west by the simmering discontent of city life. The main street opening up in front of de Leon's dusty windshield would have consisted of little more than a combination post office and general store, the storefront chapel of Our Lady of Night Blossoms, the hulking remains of the Imperium (a failed venue for theater and film), and the Misión Recursos Hotel, a two-story converted mission offering cheap long-term tenancy to the exceptional artist who managed to find his or her way there. Perhaps the mingled smells from the general store—a dank, dusty sweetness—reminded him of home. By now, he was a recently orphaned adult, and tokens of his youth would have filled him with pangs of familiarity too pleasant yet to provoke guilt. He would have recognized his own agnostic reverence in the pilgrims sitting in lotus posture before the candlelit altar of Our Lady. The shrine was one of several throughout the region, devoted to the Virgin who appeared there centuries ago to lead those lost in the desert with blossoms that shone with the brilliance of stars, even on moonless nights. He would have inquired about lodging at the general store and, when pointed toward the Misión Recursos, enjoyed a prospect of sandstone bluffs and piñon trees backlit by a waxing moon.

The lobby was dimly lit. As he approached the lone clerk, he could hear hoots in the distance, accompanied by drumbeats and the tentative tuning of strings. "Weekly bonfire," explained the clerk from behind a weathered copy of *Catcher in the Rye*. "Hope you're a deep sleeper." He set the book down to attend to his guest. His voice crackled through the sediment and smoke of years, but his clean-shaven face looked significantly younger. "Everyone calls me the Friar," he said. "And this is my humble parish." He drew a series of crosses in the air with his right hand, dispensing mock benedictions to a pair of lime green couches, several shelves of worn paperbacks, a television console whose cumbersome antenna had been replaced by a portable turntable and two boxes of neatly filed 45s, and an iguana behind glass, its head obscured by a plastic American astronaut planting the terrarium's surface with the Stars and Stripes.

De Leon introduced himself as the music outside began in earnest. "It'll last as long as the liquor. Why don't you help us finish it off so we can get to bed early?" The artist agreed and went to retrieve his supplies and duffle. "Need a hand?" asked the clerk. As he moved forward to help, he knocked his reading over the edge of the desk. De Leon stooped to pick up the paperback spread flat on the freshly swept tiles. A smaller volume was concealed within its pages. De Leon retrieved the black leather booklet, recognizing the red-rimmed pages and thumb index of a pocket New Testament.

* * *

The Friar was an excellent cook within the narrow constraints of his bachelor's repertoire. After a full day of work—starting before dawn to avail himself of the salmon and eggshell-blue light of sunrise—de Leon would join neighbors crammed around the Friar's first-floor kitchenette for omelets, pastas, and stews. The Friar offered reduced lodging for contributions to his pantry, and he never failed to distill delicacies from the general store's happenstance provisions.

The artists toasted to progress and dormant inspiration. They shared stories of their experiences abroad trailing mentors, patrons, and lovers. They debated politics fiercely and knowledgeably (the specter of a Nixon presidency, the consensus agreed, would be enough to bring voters to their senses in the fall). It was at the Friar's table that de Leon learned the history of Recursos as a lavish and doomed gift from a lovestruck tycoon to his underage mistress, whose ghost reputedly still wandered what remained of the twenty-acre resort planned in her honor, its construction cut short by her tragic (and, to some, questionable) suicide just one month shy of legal age.

In the midst of one of these freewheeling symposia, de Leon asked for his wine to be refilled. "Friar!" he shouted. He checked himself at the unwarranted blare of his voice. "*Uno más* before you cut me off." The host approached and began to pour what remained in the bottle.

"Friar," de Leon repeated. "Why do they call you the Friar?"

The wine continued to pour, but he saw his friend's hand clench briefly at the tipped bottle. The Friar retreated to the sink and began running water for dishes.

"I was a seminarian," he explained. He addressed his words to the darkened kitchen window, which reflected back an uncharacteristically pensive expression.

"You never took orders?"

The Friar shook his head. "Not the expected kind." Having dropped out before his scheduled ordination, he had waited tables for several months until drifting to Recursos. He arrived still bearing the tonsure of his order, maintained perhaps as a pledge of eventual return. His tenants continued calling him the Friar even after his hair grew out into his now familiar ponytail.

De Leon recognized a kindred ambivalence in the Friar's narrative—for would the artist himself have stumbled on Recursos if he had not been taught from infancy to expect wonders from the humble swaddling of the flesh? But the younger de Leon had long since abandoned what he considered an abject path to revelation, a tally of vices and virtues no more enlightening than the bookkeeping of his late parents. He was curious for the Friar to elaborate on his story. Alternately, he sought to express approbation for a fellow traveler. The mute expression reflected back to him invited no response. De Leon finished his drink and left.

*   *   *

With the coming of summer, the general store acquired part-time assistance from the owner's adolescent daughter. Her given name is lost to the record; she was known to her father and denizens of the Misión as Ruby, a possible play on her actual name, a reference to the distinctive light chestnut hair she shared with her father, or a reference to the corresponding ruddiness of her fair skin when sunburnt or embarrassed. De Leon, with the absentminded self-regard of the artist at work, would have recalled her, if at all, as a plain girl, nearly her father's height, dressing the store's windows with foil snowflakes at Christmas or pastel plastic eggs at Easter. Her presence on the day in question would have registered as half-heard small talk at dinner the night before. Perhaps he would have remembered a promised delivery of corn and green chiles as he watched the young girl struggle to maneuver a cumbersome basket onto the top shelf of the Misión's pantry. He would have been on his third cup of coffee, a rare but unavoidable necessity for the occasional days, like today, when the urge to sleep in overpowered any urge to create. He was likely contemplating a nap, cursing the infernal airlessness of his private bedroom at noontime and his fresher but noxious, noisy berth in the vacant barn that served as communal studio space. Perhaps his thinking out loud drew the girl's attention. As she laughed nervously into her shoulder, prompted by the utterance of language otherwise forbidden in her own house, her frail arms began to buckle, upsetting the now precariously balanced load overhead. He shook off his abstraction to help her push the drooping basket into place. She thanked him profusely, having averted a scolding and a potentially costly delay on this unusually busy morning. He smiled, nodded, and watched her hurry back to her father's store.

The rest of the day passed uneventfully. The encounter jolted him out of his sullen trance; his industry that afternoon more than made up for the morning's indolence. He ate and caroused heartily at dinner. When he retired that night, the bed seemed to sway gently from wine and a cool cross breeze issuing through his open windows. He intended to read a chapter from a tattered volume borrowed from the lobby, but he was filled with a pleasant exhaustion as soon as he propped his back to the pillow. He switched off the bedside lamp and drifted to sleep.

She appeared to him as she had by day, her arms extending toward a high shelf. He watched her rise on bare toes, exposing a torso smooth as cream. She turned toward him and smiled over her shoulder. He was at her side instantly, but instead of the tipping basket, he saw only her fingers gripping the empty shelf overhead. He glanced down at the niche formed by her neck and shoulders; above the taut strap of her sundress, her expression creased in frank invitation. His hands wandered to the smoothness of her belly, then to her skirt, which yielded to his urgency with a single tear. He buried his fingers in the slick cleft of her thighs, professing in a language that tore strangely from his throat.

His own voice summoned him to consciousness. The walls of his room were a sulfurous yellow, the sun long risen. Outside, he heard a workbench being moved into the shade for lunch. Realizing the time, he threw off the clammy linens of his bed and felt the floor burn his bare feet. He squinted down at the glaring tiles and saw that he was naked.

His late appearance at the barn that afternoon was noted with amusement; his perplexity was misread as a hangover. Glad for an excuse, he soon abandoned his easel for what fresh air could be found at this time of day in Recursos. What no one knew was that everything he handled that day—the moist bristle of a brush against his skin, the warm pallor of the blank canvas in front of him—returned him viscerally to the night before.

He walked south, past the windswept awnings of Main Street. At the threshold of the general store, he was relieved to find the proprietor by himself behind the cash register, bartering for credit with a sculptor of stone. The alley branching to his right was cast in shadow; he felt refreshed by a sudden coolness. Half a block ahead, he recognized the back entrance of the abandoned Imperium. He had never been inside. The Misión's conceptual contingent often looted the premises for collages and installations. He found the door nailed shut, but the bottom half had been sawn out and propped haphazardly over the disused doorway.

He stooped through and found himself walking a plush corridor feebly illuminated from the opening behind him. It occurred to him that he needed a flashlight, but he could distinctly see the outlines of seats in the distance. He emerged into a vacant auditorium, raked by light from the stage. From where he stood, he could see the splintered edge of where the roof had collapsed, driven in by years of sparse but torrential rain. Despite this, the stage had been picked clean. He was mildly startled by the entrance from the wings of a tall youth wearing a dark suit that was slightly long at the cuffs. He did not seem surprised at de Leon's presence; rather, he seemed to welcome an audience. "How do I look?" he said gruffly from the middle of the stage.

De Leon laughed as the boy's large fedora slipped over his forehead and down onto his nose. "Ready for Broadway," he said.

The boy made his way to the edge of the stage with striking grace. As he paced, the cuffs of his trousers revealed bare toes. He stopped and bowed. The fedora plummeted into the orchestra pit, revealing long strands of hair that flamed orange in the proscenium's light. Standing again at full height, the proprietor's daughter peered in disappointment over the edge.

"Shoot," she softly exclaimed.

The shock of the girl's transformation was exceeded for de Leon only by the evenness of his voice. "You shouldn't be here by yourself. What if you'd fallen in?"

She bristled coyly at his question, her cheeks flushed as she responded. "I wouldn't've."

De Leon noticed he was standing up. He watched her toes flex at the edge of the stage. "That's a long way down," he said.

"I've jumped from higher." She squatted. He could hear the sift of her costume as it stretched at the haunches. "There's a nice breeze from the basement if you lie down just right."

"You sleep here?"

She nodded. "It's better than sweating in bed at home. Everything smells like that store." She bit her nails pensively, then looked abruptly overhead at the collapsed roof. Lengthening shadows crossed her freckled cheeks. "I'm supposed to help with supper." She ran to the wings. De Leon heard the whine of a zipper as she hastily changed clothes.

"Does your dad know about this place?"

She emerged in a loose shift printed with tiny pink and blue flowers. "He doesn't have to," she said. She smiled at him and began binding her hair into a folded kerchief.

"No," de Leon answered, "he doesn't." He watched her retreat down the darkened corridor.

* * *

She appeared to him that night wearing her hair in a single braid down her back. He watched his fingers undo the lilac ribbon and tease apart the woven strands. She laughed as his hands worked, brushing the back of her neck. Her loosened hair fell over his fingers; his thumb wavered at the line of her jaw. She turned into his grip, suckling the edge of his palm. He pulled her by the throat to his mouth; one bare breast rose against the stiffness of a cloak. He buried his arms beneath its folds. She struggled as he wrapped himself over her nakedness. He felt her flinch at the scrape of his stubble between her breasts. He took one in his mouth and bit into the nipple. He awoke to the heat of another midday, his mouth and pillow crusted with blood.

He could not dissemble a second night without sleep. His distraction and irritation were evident; he passed the day in a feeble performance of his craft. He would have avoided his bed that night, despite an exhaustion that seemed to grind his muscles into the earth of the vacant streets. He approached the still lit storefront of Our Lady of Night Blossoms, where he found the Friar using a taper to light the last in a row of squat red candles. The flames wavered slightly before the statue of the Virgin, robed in crimson and silver on the topmost shelf of a modest altar. If he had noticed de Leon's earlier vexation at dinner, he said nothing as he blew out the taper. He acknowledged the artist with an embarrassed nod, as if caught in the performance of an elaborate and until now private compulsion.

For a time, de Leon could think of nothing to say. Finally, he broke the silence. "Do you ever miss it?"

"Miss what?"

De Leon nodded vaguely at the shrine and spent taper. The Friar shrugged.

"I used to want to be a priest." De Leon had never told this to anyone, not even his parents.

"Really?"

"When I was younger. A lot younger. It was like having magic powers. God pouring out your fingers at baptisms. Communions." *Exorcisms*, he thought, remembering the agonies of the night before.

The Friar turned to de Leon, as if reading his mind. "That's not how it works," he said.

"Well, sure, I know that."

The Friar grasped him firmly by the shoulders. "The devil never gives you a choice." He stared briefly at de Leon before pocketing his matches.

* * *

On the third night, he saw nothing but darkness and then a wedge of blue light. He mounted a set of stairs and saw her sleeping form in the silvery distance. Wind rippled the sheet draped loosely up to her shoulders. She rolled to one side, taking the sheet with her. He saw the quilting of a sleeping bag, which had left an ornate imprint on her bare

The Devil and the Dairy Princess

back. The markings ended at the band of cotton briefs that jutted thinly over her exposed hip. He stood before her, watching her sleep. In the curl of her lips as she breathed, he recognized the simpering concessions of previous nights; he smiled, suspecting the pretense of her light snores. He lowered his hand. He could feel the heat of her breath on his fingers. He was undoing the front of his jeans with his other hand when a pale flutter crossed the edge of his vision. He withdrew just as the girl's startled silhouette rose from the floor. She clutched the sheet tightly to her chest and craned her neck into the darkness behind her. He remained long enough to watch her lie back and resume the stillness of a vision, which tonight was not a vision. Gradually, the evenness of her breathing receded behind him.

Sobbing, he emerged once more into the alley behind the Imperium. A moon lidded by clouds rendered the streets of Recursos indistinct to his eyes. He stumbled to the nearest source of light. The Misión was only three short blocks up the street, but as he peered into the candlelit window of Our Lady of Night Blossoms, his legs felt impossibly heavy. He forced his way into the vestibule and found himself before the shrine. The Virgin of the desert night regarded him blankly. From the wideness of her empty gaze and the thickness of her lashes, de Leon saw that she was merely a child's doll, rendered an icon by the application of a red felt cape and a wire crown pasted with sequins. He could see the cherubic girth of its plastic belly peering through a gap in the material. He stared past the icon at the moonless blank outside. He dropped to his knees before the illuminated void, his lips shaping themselves at first awkwardly, then with greater authority, around the first words of the Lord's Prayer.

The Devil and the Dairy Princess

Toward the end of the nineteenth century, in the upstate village of Eligius, a dairy farmer, whose name has been lost to posterity, broke off from his labors to rest. This particular day in early summer was unusually cool. Mist roiled over the pasture as his herd tore at the moist turf. Perhaps it was the farmer's exhaustion that imbued the herd with a strange intransigence. Jaws pulsed blindly in the thickening mist; flanks shifted and twitched in unsettling congruence as if at any moment, the obscurity would part to reveal the bloated paunch of a prehistoric grotesque. The farmer was apprehending, unreined from industry, the grim alchemy of ruminant digestion, eternal consumption, eternal expulsion, a bestial indifference that had existed since the first dawn, and would doubtless supplant the most monumental of human designs. He recalled the admonition about work and idle hands, but too late to escape the approach of enormous hooves. The hooves supported a pair of enormous legs, a dark topcoat, and a bowler hat drawn low over the eyes.

A leathery hand pawed the side of the choicest milker. "Handsome specimen," remarked a deep voice, which seemed to reach the farmer from high in the curdling mist.

The farmer was at first too afraid to protest as the hand descended to cup the teats. "Who are you?" he finally managed.

"A harbinger," responded the voice, dispatching him to fetch the Reverend Jonah Cooper immediately for an audience. If the messenger felt any indignation at the speaker's presumption, it was impossible to discern from the urgency of his steps toward town.

Reverend Cooper was just settling in for his afternoon nap when he was roused by pounding at the rectory door. He did little to hide his irritation with the waiting messenger, who seemed nevertheless oblivious to the reverend's displeasure. Cooper followed the farmer reluctantly to his pasture.

They arrived to a circle of bovines, legs tented in obeisance to a hulking silhouette in their midst. The figure scratched idly at a raised muzzle. The reverend appraised the assembled supplicants, the tenebrous shade of the stranger's clothes, the amused bellow that resonated through the earth as a calf lapped hungrily at an outstretched palm arrayed with oddly attenuated fingers.

"Pardon me," the visitor said. "I have my followers, as you have yours."

"No one follows me," the reverend responded. "We follow the Lord."

"I'm pleased to hear that," answered the visitor, who now stood and approached the wooden barrier between them. Below the hat's brim, the reverend could discern a bulbous forehead and neatly trimmed beard.

"What is it you want?" asked the reverend.

"Your impertinence surprises me," replied the visitor. "I find it hard to believe that you, of all people, need instruction on civility from one such as I. Allow me all the same to introduce myself—"

"I know who you are," Cooper replied.

"Well, of course you do. How silly of me. I find your weekly insights from the pulpit quite enlightening. They are, in fact, the reason I'm here."

"Go on," said the reverend.

Thus revealed, the Devil explained that he was ready to admit defeat. He had been flushed out by the citizens of this, the godliest part of the country. He could no longer depend on subterfuge if his quarry were so alert to the usual tricks. So he had decided to conduct his business out in the open, like any tradesman. He still required sustenance, certainly, but he now had no choice but to yield to the contingencies of predation, culling only the weakest and least necessary. He would endure eternity on the leavings that were his due, while those who prevailed would be left in peace to pursue the New Jerusalem.

Reverend Cooper craned his neck to look the creature right in its eyes. He could not find them and instead settled his stalwart gaze on the dark space veiled by the bowler's brim. "What then," asked the reverend, "do you propose?"

"To be your humble servant," answered the Devil. The people of Eligius would be granted prosperity for all their earthly days, until the Lord of all returned to claim his kingdom. All that was required in exchange was one soul per year, of the town's choosing, in whatever manner the good people deemed fit. And there was an exception even for these minimal terms: for should the offered sacrifice be pure in heart and spirit, the Devil would be rendered powerless to enforce his part of the contract and required to hunt for souls elsewhere, leaving the town's abundance intact as a token of righteous victory.

No town had as yet been courageous enough to accept. The Devil shook his head in disappointment, running scaled fingers over a splintery fence beam. He had been greeted with skepticism throughout his travels, but more often with fear disguised as humility. For many, the thriving of future generations was no solace for the loss of a single soul to the demon's minions. And who could claim the purity required to successfully breach the bargain once made? So had gone countless encounters over numerous miles. Was there no community that actually lived by the faith declared in song every Sunday? Surely somewhere there must be believers willing to allow him the little that was his due, or to challenge him altogether for even this pittance?

Reverend Cooper could not help but be flattered. He was well aware of the biblical interdiction against testing the Lord. But this wasn't really testing the Lord, was it? Really, it was he himself being tested, along with all who claimed allegiance to the Lord's teachings. What if, in fact, this test had been arranged by the Lord himself to measure the worthiness of his flock? A new century was imminent and with it, perhaps a new urgency to fulfill the visions of Scripture.

"What say you, Reverend?" asked the Devil, extending his left hand.

The reverend, saying nothing, reached for the offered claw. His fingers caught on one of the demon's long, flinty nails. Blood poured from the wound, seeping into the earth below.

Cooper returned to town just in time for dinner, where he regaled his family with the tale of his otherworldly bargain. Abigail Cooper, for her part, relished every detail of her husband's triumph, flinching only briefly at the announcement that the inaugural sacrifice would be their eldest daughter, Theresa. The reverend, seeing anxiety trace itself across his wife's brow and the faces of their six children, was too sated with purpose to admonish them. He took Theresa's hand and assured her that no harm would come to her. He knew that her sacrifice would be untenable under the terms of the bargain. If Theresa wept as she accepted her father's will, it was surely feminine frailty and not the pliancy of faith that betrayed her.

The appointed hour arrived. The people were instructed to wait at the border of the surrounding woods for the reverend's signal, which would let them know that all were safe. The combatants entered the moonlit forest goaded by hymns and spontaneous acclamations. Jonah Cooper lit the way with his torch, followed by his daughter and Nelson Flynn, whose proposal of marriage Theresa had just accepted. Refusing to let his fiancée weather this trial without him, he entered the woods bearing the carved oak cross that had crowned the steeple of Eligius's church for nearly two centuries. Those gathered watched Reverend Cooper's flame fade slowly into the shadows. When it was gone altogether, they linked hands and prayed, first for their reverend, who had brought them fearlessly to the threshold of redemption, and then in thanksgiving for the souls of Nelson and Theresa and their generous sacrifice, which was not really a sacrifice at all if one was truly blessed by faith, which they assuredly were. They prayed for the pending marriage of Nelson and Theresa, that it would be blessed with prosperity and love and abundant progeny. They prayed for the progeny of Nelson and Theresa, that they would always remember this day, when the seeds of their bright and abundant future were sown. There was a brief pause as several of the assembly looked into the darkened woods, where the promised signal had yet to appear. They were quickly wrenched back from distraction by calls to pray for the coming prosperity that would result from the present trial, that it might be used prudently and always in keeping with the spiritual guidance that had led them to prevail. A deep rustle within the forest dampened the chorus of amens; a pair of broad white wings rose from the branches overhead and veiled the dwindling moon. Perhaps it would be prudent to pray for the nation as a whole? asked one of the faithful through a shiver that tensed her shoulders. Yes, agreed the wavering circle, hands numbed by frost. One wouldn't want to forget the nation.

Before the nation could be blessed, however, a bright light flared in the distance. The exhausted assembly squinted to ensure that this was no illusion. Indeed, the light persisted and spread, edging a trail through the dense trunks. The people cheered and followed the light, laughing as they stumbled over unseen roots or felt the slap of low branches. They emerged into a clearing about a mile into the forest. A large, elliptical stone rose vacantly at its center. To the left of the stone, a figure crouched in the light of blinding flames, shifting feebly on its knees, hands outstretched. A neighbor recognized the reverend and rushed to help him. Cooper made no effort to stand, despite his rescuer's appeals; instead, the reverend turned his face to the stunned gathering and screamed through the bloody maw that remained of his mouth. The flames doused themselves, revealing what was left of the town cross.

* * *

The Devil and the Dairy Princess

So began the long-standing détente between the Devil and the people of Eligius, who, at the very least, were never betrayed by the surviving party. The town's fortunes rose steadily into the next century, even as those of the nation waned. Through Dust Bowl and Great Depression, not a single of Eligius's fields lay fallow; its herds boasted record milk production. The vague sulfur taste, attributed to local innovations in the science of feed, could be substantially mellowed during pasteurization, and some experts found the raw flavor essential to the area's finer cheeses. Over the years, the sacrifice in the woods took on the fanciful implausibility of myth or senility as witnesses aged and went on to an afterlife that, they could only hope, offered the solace of annihilating sleep. The Eligius they left behind had always been a fertile oasis in the wilderness, always producing for those with the vigor and resilience to tame the land. The people had always taken pride in their work, always tempered with the humility to recognize their debt to divine Providence. And every June, always the week before the nation celebrated its independence, the town celebrated the bounty of the preceding year by electing one of its own to promote dairy products to surrounding communities.

The post of dairy princess was among the most coveted in the region, unless you were one of the four community elders apprised of its actual purpose. Since the mysterious disappearance of Theresa Cooper and her fiancé in the summer of 1894—a likely elopement, of course, youth having always been so impetuous—discretion was required to sustain the original bargain. The Dairy Commission convened formally for the first time in the autumn of 1901; its four lifetime appointees were primarily responsible for enforcing the rules of election and assuring neglect by the public and press. The closest call in the commission's history came in the winter of 1972, when a reporter for the *Barrettown Bugle* began investigating a sizeable payment made by the then-mayor of Eligius to the contest coordinator, who subsequently eliminated the mayor's seventeen-year-old daughter from competition due to questionable interpretation of an obscure bylaw. The daughter's outrage—this was her last year of eligibility after a string of disappointing placements as second and third runner-up—was quickly assuaged with the promise of a new car. The *Bugle* reporter, however, was not so easily deterred, even after receiving a parcel with a Washington, DC, postmark during the first week of August. Had the reporter actually opened the parcel, the contents would have at least merited a one-inch squib in the "Washington Roundup" column toward the back of section A: inside was a blank sheet of White House stationary sleeved around an unmarked reel of audiotape. Before the reporter could reach for his letter opener, however, circumstance intervened when word reached the bureau that a dog had fallen through the ice at Brasher Inlet; in the ensuing rush to the scene and two weeks of spot and follow-up coverage—the dog survived—the sealed package was lost and never recovered.

The rest of the commission's responsibilities involved planning the annual coronation ceremony. Reverend Cooper lived to see the dedication of Theresa Cooper Pavilion in 1954; the pavilion, financed by the first group of commissioners, boasted dark neoclassical columns, a white marble floor inlaid with gold, and an elaborate pastoral frieze animated by the dimmest moonlight. Cooper made a comical dignitary as he dozed through remarks by the mayor and a medley of patriotic favorites performed a cappella by the local Tonic Tillers. The reverend had not slept a full night since his daughter started visiting him shortly after her assumption into the underworld. It wasn't so bad, she would assure him, crossing the sleeves of her loose crimson gown, her face scarred by the shadows of maple branches. Her master was quite solicitous, actually, and very understanding about her early deficiencies as a spouse. She had since been amply instructed, she added, looking at the lush lawns outside. By the way his daughter shifted slightly in her stance, the way her garment gathered and hung over her bare feet, he knew she was naked underneath. He keened over the stump of his tongue, an attempt to ask after her mother, who had died in her sleep in the early spring of 1902. He never got the chance to find out, always waking alone in the darkness of his room.

At the subsequent dedication reception—which set the standard for all subsequent Dairy Court dinners—the reverend was congratulated by a representative of the Dairy Commission. Despite the humidity of the April afternoon, the representative wore a dark three-piece suit. His brow was dry as it brushed idly against the bunting strung

The Devil and the Dairy Princess

along the pavilion's Corinthian capitals. He looked down at the progenitor of Eligius's great fortune and extended a hand in greeting. Cooper gripped the armrests of his seat. Age had done little to improve his manners, the representative mused. He gave the reverend's shoulders a brusque, encouraging shake and complimented his wisdom in choosing the Devil he knew. That night, Reverend Cooper at last chose the one he didn't; his housekeeper and sometime nurse discovered him the following morning, hanging from a second-story handrail.

The turn of the subsequent century introduced a new fervor among Eligians, who perhaps had always lived with the guilt of easeful existence, even if its actual source was never widely known. The prospect of a new millennium was seen by many as an opportunity for repentance or the consoling excess that precedes apocalypse. Something of both was heard in the sermons of Terry Dillon, an excommunicated priest who proudly enumerated the dozen countries where he had performed exorcisms, a practice restricted by the obfuscating bureaucracy of a Vatican that Dillon saw as irredeemably corrupt. His Church of the Exorcism was only radical if one accepted the dilution to which all the major faiths had succumbed in recent years; he and his followers were merely witnesses to a truth too many had forgotten: evil was only as inherent as the common cold or grippe. The expulsion from Eden was ultimately a side effect of the poison ingested and passed on by Eve. But it was pointless to continue blaming the weakness of woman, however deserved. The defeat of the Devil now depended on purging him by increments through the sacrament of exorcism. Every Sunday, the faithful of Eligius would gather in an abandoned granary to share reports of suspicious behavior witnessed in a given week. Incidences of strange disturbance, particularly at the wooded fringes of town, convinced parishioners that the demon was indeed in their midst. Dillon led them to the desolate edges of Eligius every first night of the full moon to chant and pray in warning to whatever creatures dared to breach the beams of their storm lanterns. The darkness yielded owls, skunks, the occasional raccoon, but no sign of the promised quarry. The former priest raised both arms, lantern hooked loosely on his outstretched thumb. Never mind, he admonished; vigilance would, in time, be its own reward. His admirers nodded, squinting into the sway of light.

Agnes Hadley fell in step behind her mother as the procession made its way back to town. Georgina Hadley was exchanging marble cake recipes with one of her fellow tellers at the AgroBank branch on lower Main when she saw her daughter dragging her steps. For the parishioners of the Church of the Exorcism, tonight was one skirmish closer to Revelation; for the rest of Eligius, it was a Friday. Music and neon light ascended from the distant doors of both of the town's legal drinking establishments. Once over the glossy thresholds, the light and noise were muffled by the starless expanse above. At Agnes's age, Georgina would have followed the boots and high heels, the music and cigarette smoke, the drunken laughter and fumbling at damp dollar bills. But this was how she had met Agnes's father, and she was determined that her daughter cultivate early a fervor for moderation, distilled of the passions that, inevitably, taunt us longer in recollection than in real life. She commanded Agnes to rejoin the group immediately.

There was little danger of Agnes losing her way. She had none of Georgina's sensuality, which even now took effort to disguise under drab suits and opaque stockings. Agnes was so unlike her mother that town gossips often spent slower weeks revisiting rumors of her adoption. Agnes was more her father's child, a muddy brunette with flat features and a parsimonious figure no dress could enliven. Glasses might have given her face much needed character, but excellent vision was the one perfection Agnes did possess, and Georgina refused to even look at the fashionable cosmetic lenses recommended by friends at school.

The Hadleys returned home from their monthly patrol to find their front door open and a pair of black loafers crossed casually in the dimness of the porch light. Xerxes, their 180-pound mastiff, barked feebly at the seated stranger from the shadowy vestibule. The barking grew louder when he spotted his masters walking hesitantly up the narrow driveway; Xerxes continued to sound his alarm as he bolted over the front lawn and crouched anxiously behind them. While Agnes tried to calm the dog, Georgina withdrew her phone from her purse and took the three steps remaining to the open door.

"The door was unlocked," the stranger said. "I hope you don't mind."

The Devil and the Dairy Princess

Georgina certainly did mind, but when she tried to express her anger, she found herself incapable of speech. Her grip slackened on the phone, which dropped to the floor and skidded to a stop against her guest's reflective shoes. The stranger stood and introduced himself as a representative of the Dairy Commission.

By now, Agnes had managed to coax the mastiff to the threshold of the house and was struggling to bring him in again by the collar. There was a snap and a scatter of pads across the vestibule floor. Agnes emerged into the living room, staring at the torn collar hanging limp in her hand.

The dairy representative stepped toward the door and helpfully closed it behind her. "Almost had him," he said, with a wink. "You must have some grip."

"I guess," said Agnes. She recognized the tricolor pentacle on his lapel pin and froze, suddenly conscious of her disheveled appearance and the wet earthy smell Xerxes had left on her face and hands.

"I was just telling your mother how much we look forward to seeing you for registration at the pavilion next week."

"You were?" Agnes looked at her mother.

"Agnes was sick last year. That's why—"

"Of course," said the representative. "You were right to keep her at home. Our bylaws are very clear on the need for all contestants to be in peak health. But your daughter looks quite eligible now." He was distracted briefly by the dark hairs visible across the girl's upper lip.

"With all due respect, Mr. . . . ."

He nodded agreeably. "I'm with the commission." He resumed his seat on the faded floral lounger.

"Yes. . . . As I was saying, my daughter and I aren't really interested in your competition."

"But a girl—young woman—has only three precious years of eligibility to represent Eligius. It would be a shame to see her miss yet another opportunity."

Georgina looked at her daughter. "I know what an opportunity this is. I was third runner-up to Beatrice Watson a few years back."

"Congratulations! The commission still remembers that as one of the most difficult years to judge. So many worthy candidates."

"I remember. A shame what happened. Did Bea ever get better?"

The representative shook his head. "Overdose, I'm afraid. Not two months after she was crowned."

"I thought she was getting help."

"Oh, she was," the representative insisted. "The commission never turns its back on one of its own. We spared no expense. We thought she would benefit from one of the more remote treatment programs. Unfortunately . . . well, I can't say more without violating our obligations to the Watson family."

"Of course," said Georgina. She contemplated an empty seat opposite the representative, but she could not get her knees to bend. She tried dissembling her awkward stance by brushing at dust specks on the mantle. "They say it's cursed," she said, her back to the room.

"What is?"

"All of it. The crown. The contest. Ever since I was a girl."

The representative emerged at full height from the lounger.

"Make no mistake," the representative said evenly. "Winning is a serious responsibility that should never be assumed lightly. Some are elected and recognize ambitions in themselves they would never before dare admit. Others come to appreciate the seriousness of their position and begin to question their worthiness. And sometimes, though not often, some take their questioning too far. That's understandable, isn't it?"

Georgina nodded. The representative regarded her a few moments before turning to Agnes.

"The world is changing," he observed. "The commission believes the post should reflect these changes. We stress—have always stressed—that this is not a beauty contest. Or, rather, the beauty we assess can manifest in any number of ways. Tell me, Agnes, what do you dream of doing?"

Agnes's grin revealed a spackling of strawberry pulp from that night's dessert. "I never really remember my dreams."

The representative chuckled amiably. "A sense of humor," he said. "Another plus in the eyes of the judges. But seriously, dear, what do you dream of accomplishing? In the future? You strike me as one of those shy girls who end up discovering a cure for something. Still waters and all that."

Agnes grew nervous. "I don't know," she answered, staring at her shoes. She tamped at a dog-eared corner of the living room rug. The corner rose stubbornly despite her efforts.

"Certainly," said the representative as he stooped to smooth the carpet by hand. "You choose to live in the moment. I wish we all had such free spirits. Your daughter has the soul of a poet," he added, just before his hand was crushed under Agnes's ill-timed heel.

Georgina was roused from her strange stupor by the familiar need to correct her daughter's clumsiness. She helped the representative up and guided him back to his seat, apologizing profusely. Agnes was too embarrassed to join her mother; she froze in place, ensuring that the offending foot would cause no more damage. The representative resumed his seat and made a tentative fist.

"Are you sure you're all right? Agnes Marie, go get this man some ice."

"No. Please. That won't be necessary."

"It's the least she can do. I insist. Agnes—"

The representative opened his hand and raised it in dismissal. Not until the night of her daughter's coronation would Georgina remember how strangely his fingers met the air, his nails trimmed acutely, the pads curling slightly at the tips, like beads of flame from a stove burner turned low.

He asked Agnes to hand him his briefcase. With his good hand, he slowly undid the latches and withdrew a densely printed form, thick with carbons. There was no need to apologize, he assured them. Accidents happen. But the secret of success was knowing the difference between accident and opportunity. Avoiding the former merely prolonged the interval between unavoidable obstacles. Avoiding the latter condemned one to a life of mediocrity and regret. Surely this was not the fate Georgina Hadley wished for her daughter? Agnes tried to conceal her growing excitement as her mother took the offered papers.

* * *

The transformation of Agnes Hadley was as subtle as it was unexpected. Cosmetics did not conceal and soften her imperfections so much as imbue them with a gaudy polish. If she maintained absolutely rigid posture, the fit of her gown appeared, from the right angle, almost flattering. She had never fallen testing her mother's heels on her own feet, although she never did master the glide the judges looked for in evaluating poise; at her most practiced, Agnes's steps were as sound as the bovines with whom she would be sharing the stage over the next year. Her biggest challenge, after the "Whey Out Dairy Facts" quiz bowl, would be the second-round extemporaneous speech on a randomly assigned industry topic. The three-minute time was strictly enforced, and many promising candidates succumbed to nervous stammering or baffled silence as the warning light went from green to amber at two minutes and thirty seconds. Regretting her consent the moment the Dairy Commission representative vanished into the darkness between tree trunks, Georgina watched helplessly as her daughter vacillated between paralyzing doubt and feverish hope.

The evening of the competition, a dozen candidates approached their respective podiums at Cooper Pavilion. From Agnes's place onstage, the audience was a field of banners and camera flashes. Four judges were visible as featureless silhouettes in the foreground. Agnes felt the stare of the tallest silhouette and could even make out the faintest of nods in her direction as the mayor of Eligius took the stage.

Whether quizzed on "Lactose Lore," "Bovine Biology," "Milk in History," or "Icons and Innovators," Agnes answered with an unaccustomed confidence, placing second overall and easily winning a berth in the next round. She was a competent student, but her disquisition on the twenty-first-century dairy alluded to pending advances familiar only to specialists. Her question during the third and final interview round ("Why do you want to be Dairy Princess?") was considered one of the most difficult to answer with zeal and originality at this late stage of the competition. But once again, Agnes proved herself a knowledgeable and engaging promoter of dairy to a community that needed to go back to nutritional and moral basics. By now, she had the crowd substantially on her side. Georgina Hadley watched from a seat five rows back as her daughter finished her interview to whistles and a standing ovation. She humbly nodded, acknowledging the looks of other parents who recognized her as Agnes's mother. She allowed herself a glance or two at the expressions of approval and envy that typically marked such occasions. But the looks she was given were strangely muted, edged with something else that she told herself was inscrutable.

By the time of the coronation, the crowd's cheers took on an avid expectancy. The mayor shouted into his wireless microphone his thanks to all the contestants, to the judges for their judiciousness, to the Dairy Commission for all its hard work, and to the community for its attendance and commitment to local industry before dismissing them all with promises of next year's spectacle. The stage behind him was vacant. Georgina watched her daughter's tiara retreat amid a coterie of shadows. The exiting crowd pushed her further back as she struggled to catch up.

She finally managed to sidle out between a pair of columns. In her rush toward a rank of departing cars, she caught someone's shoulder. She stopped to apologize and recognized Terry Dillon. Dillon tried to arrange himself into the severity appropriate to his clerical status, but he could not ignore Georgina's desperation as she excused herself and started bolting for the parking lot. Publicly, Dillon disapproved of the vanity that the annual dairy festival encouraged in the community's young women; privately, he, along with many other Eligians, was curious to see just what would result from Agnes Hadley's unlikely bid for Dairy Princess, and he was hopeful for a passing word with Georgina, whose attractions had begun to perturb him during weekly meetings at the granary. He held her fast by the shoulders and asked her what was wrong. She was distracted briefly by Dillon's boldness. Dillon, loosening his grasp, repeated his question. Georgina Hadley replied with a confused and fragmentary recitation of clues, hints, signs, and insinuations that concluded with a single tangible fact: her daughter was being taken. The pastor needed no further convincing.

In Dillon's truck, they followed a silver sedan to the border of the woods. The sedan slowed before a nondescript expanse of trees. Dillon stopped his truck discreetly behind. Georgina panicked and fumbled for the passenger door lock. Dillon grasped her hand in the darkness. He knew where they were going. Over the years, he had mapped every possible gathering space for nocturnal conspiracy. In this sector of the woods, there was only one place where they could gather, a clearing that could be accessed without detection by one or two hikers from a nearby trailhead.

They each took a flashlight, but after several minutes of gently rising terrain, these were no longer necessary. A coppery aura illuminated their steps between gnarled roots. An opening emerged in the distance, ending in a thick trunk that seemed to bead and drip onto the crimson grass rustling below. The trunk detached itself from the surrounding trees and reached the prostrate form of Agnes Hadley in two strides.

The figure stood over his prize and hooked her tiara with a single claw. He threw the bauble into the grass with disgust. How he hated when his due was delivered in the finery of mortal hands. He preferred them natural, unadorned. He yoked Agnes's face between two fingers and lifted her to her feet. Her cheeks were streaked with blood where his rough skin abraded hers.

The Devil hesitated. "Are you feeding these things?" he asked, turning to the four suited silhouettes waiting at the edge of the clearing. "This one looks a little . . . small. Never understood the fashion for starving. Very well, then."

This being the one soul he could claim for the entire year, he had to consume it with appropriate ceremony. He began with a mock recitation of baptismal vows. "Tell me," he began, "do you believe in the one true Lord who guided your forefathers in the extension of his great work?" For every affirmative answer, spoken in the agonies of last hope, he would tear at layers of clothing and skin, until the soul was relieved to his possession.

To Agnes Hadley, death was a romantic abstraction, as palpable and solemn as a window-dressing Father Christmas presiding at a nativity scene. She was old enough and lonely enough to have romanticized her own death, the despair of others as they mourned, which she would somehow be able to enjoy from a comfortable perch in the Great Beyond. But there was nothing of comfort in her imminent demise. She tried to swallow back the dryness in her mouth, managing only to tighten the searing noose formed at her throat by the demon's fingers. His catechismal taunts recalled to her the whisper of earth beneath the feet of Terry Dillon's disciples as they patrolled the bordering woods, their songs and Scripture dampened instantly by a great silence.

Agnes Hadley regarded the Devil's damp beard. "No," she answered. She did not.

The Devil loosened his fingers slightly but chose to ignore her whispered insolence. "Do you," he continued, "vow to live by the Creed you took at baptism for all your earthly days as witnessed by parents, proxies, and the community of faith?"

Agnes, suddenly afforded breath, answered more loudly this time, so that her voice carried to the fringes of the clearing. "No," she repeated.

The Devil, foiled in his vanity for surrender, jabbed the soft dip of her neckline and made a diagonal slash across the front of her dress. Agnes collapsed before the towering shade, which seemed to bloat slightly at the edges.

"Look at me," the Devil commanded. When Agnes did not move, he poised two fingers over her neck, but held back to resume.

"Do you vow to be always vigilant against the inroads of evil, in yourself and others, whether in word, deed, or intent?"

Agnes stood, her arms crossed over her chest. She hesitated in what at a distance resembled the guarding of wounds. But when she lowered her arms, causing the top of her dress to fall away, her skin was unbroken, its pallor changing the dark hair around her nipples to a wiry silver.

Agnes met the Devil's stare and answered a third time, "No."

At this point, extant accounts vary. For some, the ceremony in the woods coincided with a strange tumult all along Main Street. The cornices on public buildings crumbled, groceries toppled to tilting floors, likely provoked by numerous herds that escaped in panic to parts unknown, leaving many of Eligius's most productive pastures empty, as if the missing had been absorbed into the very earth itself.

Others claim that late in the long night, angels descended, their robes and swords the hue of ivory, to send the demon back for good. In some versions, the girl is rewarded for her faith—asserted bravely in the face of the Devil's torture—by bodily assumption into heaven. In others, the girl refuses to answer to the Devil altogether, vowing to answer to the Lord alone; she is martyred grotesquely before her soul is freed to its rightful home and Eligius is liberated from a century's spell.

In still other versions, Eligians rise early to an ordinary morning. The sky is only beginning to lighten to deep blue. Fresh coffee is poured into cups. A barn door is coaxed open with a reluctant grate. Routine is interrupted by a group passing by on foot. Their faces are familiar, but they regard the town's outskirts like travelers arriving from a long journey. Perhaps they have been here before, perhaps they were born and raised here, but they have been away so long that their anticipation in return is tempered by fear of all they will fail to recognize and all who will fail to recognize them. Nevertheless, they continue over the narrowing contours of dirt road, approaching the only destination at hand.

The Devil and the Dairy Princess

In the Empire of Cetaceans

The annual Pheasant Lake Psychic Fair draws upward of three hundred attendees. Most are curious, if not entirely content with their fates divined via crystals, numbers, and totem animals. A great many invest in products claiming to cure everything from insomnia and stomach upset to the human condition itself. A smaller number, believing that anxiety, aggression, and disappointment are terminal, peruse book bins containing startling revelations about the true meaning of Mayan ruins and presidential assassinations, or accounts of alien abductions by celebrities from decades past.

Those in attendance during the first weekend of August 2008 might have missed one of the fair's most unusual offerings. On Saturday morning, a single placard, printed modestly in black letters on a white background, advertised:

WHALES: THE SILENT THREAT

It was followed by a time that afternoon and a room number. The placard's starkness caused a mild buzz over that morning's continental breakfast, but it also led to some uncomfortable moments as the dozen in attendance crammed the listed venue, a hotel suite four floors above the designated meeting rooms. Roughly half the audience read the whales as threatened, humans the likeliest culprits after centuries of environmental neglect. The rest read equivalence in the intervening colon, relishing the prospect of a fair and balanced rejoinder to animal lovers. As the sides recognized each other over the murmur of respective platitudes, a young, auburn-haired woman checked her watch and straightened several piles of free literature on a foldout table installed in front of a chest of drawers. Five minutes past the scheduled start time, she stood and knocked hesitantly at the door to the bedroom. Hearing no answer, she cracked the door and spoke through the narrow opening. Her smile as she walked away stiffened with resignation.

The speaker emerged at 3:10 p.m. His first action was to approach the wall opposite the clustered audience and remove the generic seascape hanging there. He dragged the nearest end table toward the middle of the room, where he placed a slide carousel and a black three-ring binder, its corners peeling to reveal blunted cardboard beneath. The binder was covered in stickers—an orange cannabis leaf, a yellow ribbon, a smirking whale captioned PROTECT THE HUMANS, the outline of a fish sprouting legs. The speaker was well-dressed in a jacket and tie but still managed to look slovenly. Pale flecks speckled his lapels.

The first slide clicked into place:

MIXED MESSAGES

The speaker cleared his throat and took a sip of bottled water. "Mixed messages," he repeated, in a voice that aspired to bass but just managed to avoid helium-induced caricature. "If you take one thing away from all this, remember: mixed messages."

For many in the audience that day, this was indeed the extent of their understanding. The speaker, who introduced himself as Jeremy Wellfleet, claimed to have taught marine biology at the Scripps aquarium in San Diego, until circumstances forced him to take a permanent

The Devil and the Dairy Princess

leave of absence. The nature of these circumstances was never elaborated.

Wellfleet began with a survey of the earth's surface: 25 percent land, 75 percent water. Within that 25 percent, humans make up only a fraction of the countless other species populating the land. And yet over the entire planet, Wellfleet noted, we alternately presume uncontested rank or sole stewardship, which essentially amounts to the same thing, recent alarmist documentaries notwithstanding. "The truth," he quipped, "is that we are the real inconvenience." He paused then for knowing laughter that was not forthcoming.

At some point during his prelude, the slide changed to

WE ARE NOT ALONE

after which a sequence of stock images appeared that might illustrate an evening news report: a rifle-wielding militant, a cadaverous child leaning on a pink wall, a bespectacled official, eyes askance as she addressed the microphones arrayed in front of her. Wellfleet narrated a series of questions as image followed image. Why does suffering continue in a species that purportedly represents the apex of evolution? What causes our history to repeat in cycles of alienation, ostracism, persecution, and war as predictable as they are tragic? And if we could, for one moment, relinquish the pretense of mastery, benevolent or otherwise, what might we learn from our planetary brethren?

At this point, his assistant distributed several volumes to audience members; all were dream dictionaries in which readers could look up salient elements from their dreams and gloss their meanings under the corresponding alphabetized entry.

"Who has Phillips's *Annotated Dream Lore*?" Wellfleet asked. A young man, pierced through the nose and lip, raised a volume bound in olive green with a cracked brown spine. Wellfleet instructed him to read the volume's entry for WHALE. After a minute or two of turning pages, the audience member shyly announced that no such entry seemed to exist. The result was the same for Leviand's *Glossaire des rêves*, Danbury's *Reader's Guide to Dreams*, Morton's *Dream Yourself Happy*, and Wesley and Currier's *Map of Manifest Content*. Every volume lacked an entry on whales, despite assiduous documentation on the significance of aardvarks, bears, sparrows, and weasels, not to mention lost teeth and fingers, flying, and pregnancy, both male and female. The assistant collected the volumes and attention was directed once again to the improvised screen:

THE TRUE MARK OF THE PUPPET MASTER
IS HOW WELL HE CONCEALS HIS STRINGS.
—Anon

The largest brains on the planet, Wellfleet continued, belong to whales. One does not have to be a neuroscientist to understand the implications of this fact. The least intelligent whale, by extrapolation, is a genius exceeding the capacities of a da Vinci or an Einstein. Accounting for the species' much longer history and the sophistication of its communication and social systems, which human scientists are only beginning to comprehend, the reasonable and responsible observer can come to only one conclusion: we are mere squatters at the primitive frontier of an empire of cetaceans.

"Now, I know what you're thinking," Wellfleet assured as he regarded his audience over the rims of his glasses. Given the varied expressions in the room—ranging from suppressed mirth to annoyed impatience to anxious glances roaming the walls for hidden cameras— this was a claim of surprising confidence.

If one were to believe in the mastery of whales, he nevertheless went on, how could one explain their regular slaughter at the hands of their natural inferiors? This presumes that a civilization as advanced as that of cetaceans lacks dissent, a quality that marks even human civilization. Whales are no different, though they have likely done a better job answering what humans, lacking their genius, are content to designate timeless questions.

Whereas most whales, given their highly developed brains, are probably ruthless in their reasoning—had Swift studied whales instead of horses, we would have a very different concluding voyage for Gulliver—some perhaps are incapable of completely ignoring the pulse of their enormous hearts. At some point in our shared histories, these exceptions, smarter than the dumbest but far short of genius, rose to the surface to breathe, feed, and calve the natural way, refusing the aid of

The Devil and the Dairy Princess

cetacean technology shrouded for centuries in the deepest ocean canyons. These empaths, over time, came to marvel at the beauties near the surface, the kaleidoscopic order of fish in schools, the dive of seabirds stalking from above. They developed a fascination for the bipeds seen in increasing numbers on ships and distant shorelines. They were perhaps amused by humans' wonder at breaching, which for the whale is nothing more than scratching an itch or saying hello. In the seconds before resubmerging, they saw the terror in the human face, pivoting skyward at their ascent. The more sensitive whales developed tenderness for the surface dwellers. They were rewarded with spears and live dissection.

Nevertheless, the whale was not to be pitied for its curiosity and compassion. The whales we often see hunted and butchered on posters and during protests are only a small minority. Numbers suggesting endangered status are highly suspect, given whales' propensity for stealth.

"Hold on," said a skeptic, leaning forward in her seat. "I have a hard time imagining how even a single whale, much less an entire . . . civilization can hide, as it were, in plain sight." The room rippled with laughter and murmured assent. The auburn-haired assistant said something under her breath and continued to dab at the crossword folded discreetly on her lap.

Wellfleet smiled as if the skeptic had just fallen into his trap. The carousel turned to the next slide:

ALIENS IN OUR MIDST

The subsequent slide featured the iconic image of alien life reported in countless abduction narratives and recycled on film and television: a bulbous gray head over an infantile body, the limbs hanging feebly like flippers. Wellfleet reassured the audience that he was not about to begin fulminating on an alien conspiracy that somehow brought his disparate points together. "This isn't the movies," he said. "If only things were that simple. Or that complicated." According to Wellfleet, the only aliens that actually existed—within the constraints of human consciousness, at any rate—were terrestrial. He forwarded the carousel with a flourish. The alien was now superimposed onto an anatomical diagram of a sperm whale, its enormous brain centered behind the alien's dark eyeholes. A humpback came next, its flippers aligned with the alien's feathery hand. Then came an orca, a beluga, and a narwhal captioned by an anonymous eyewitness:

> I WAS THEN PROBED FOR AN INDETERMINATE NUM-BER OF HOURS BEFORE I WAS RELEASED. AS THE ALIEN CRAFT TOOK OFF, IT LEFT A BROAD BLUE STREAK IN THE SKY THAT RIPPLED LIKE WATER.

Why were whales abducting humans, implanting false memories of extraterrestrial excursions? Why were they indulging our false mastery of the planet by assuming the status of endangered species? Scientists and consultants working for forward-thinking nonprofits—here, Wellfleet circulated a laminated page from *The Global Examiner*—had conclusively mapped the evolution of man in the next million years, culminating in a homunculus consisting almost entirely of brain matter that could travel by mental projection and communicate telepathically. The whale doubtless already had such capabilities, suggesting that the species was far from innocent.

In ancient Rome, emperors created entire worlds for their amusement, filling coliseums with water for mock sea battles, planting jungles within arms' reach of screaming plebeians, who wagered on which gladiator would survive the sheer cliffs and poisonous vines, the stalking lions and charging rhinos sprouting at will from under hidden doors.

At birth, the human body reveals a marvelous possibility: 25 percent solid, 75 percent water, the same proportion that gave rise to the planet's real masters, who perhaps used the same formula to mark our species as its own creation.

As long as humans are content to remain among the planet's lower species, the whales will continue their elusive plans. But, Wellfleet surmised, if we could show them how far we've come, perhaps we could rise in their estimation—never enough, of course, for them to share all their secrets, but perhaps enough to safeguard our status as a largely autonomous cetacean territory, still liable for a cut of valued resources as tribute, and still under the ultimate authority of their governing council. (Whales, Wellfleet explained, were too reasonable to be dictators but also too intelligent to rely on a completely committee-based bureaucracy; thus a single body of multiple governors was the likely structure of their political system.) What we lost in independence, we would gain in access to discoveries that, however rudimentary to our masters, might ease and even cure any number of human maladies.

The wall framed a diagram of the human brain. Wellfleet paused to trace the path of the medulla oblongata, the cerebellum, and the corpus callosum with his index finger. "Pathetic, really," he mused. "Everything we think and feel comes from this puddle of flesh circuits. Our dreams. Our nightmares. But this . . . this is *our* ocean. We can continue to tread water within reach of safe shores. Or we can sound it like the whale and see how deep it goes."

He went on to explain sounding, a technique he had pioneered—patent pending—to cultivate the brain's capacity to process and synthesize information. Human experience was hopelessly linear and compartmentalized, as shown on Wellfleet's penultimate slide:

LOWER-ORDER NEEDS
"I'm hungry"→ Seek food→ Find food→ Eat

HIGHER-ORDER NEEDS
"I'm lonely"→ Seek companionship→ Find companionship→ Socialize

"But what if," Wellfleet proposed, indicating the diagram above, "you could go from this . . . to *this*." The wall seemed to turn orange. On closer inspection, however, the solid color was in fact a mesh of lines that crossed and recrossed. Points of intersection were labeled with letters, numbers, and mathematical symbols; some areas seemed to project in larval protuberances from the wall. Wellfleet offered to explain his secret in a series of weekend workshops that cost a mere $400 for a complete month, which included materials and meals for the first two weekends.—(Participants would typically require little to no food for the remainder of the month.) A handful remained to browse the literature table.

The following November, a jogger awoke for his usual early morning run along the shore of Easton Bay, Maryland. At about the midpoint of his five-mile regimen, he stumbled and hit his shin against something soft but solid. Cursing, he regained his balance and turned to look at what tripped him in the purpling sand. It was a knapsack full of papers and graphs. Next to the bag, he saw a worn brown wallet. When the jogger leaned over to pick it up, he noticed other shapes from which sand sifted into the rising tide. There were purses, briefcases, and more wallets, one of which belonged to a James R. Wellfleet, whose expired California driver's license was the only clue to its owner. Police, following an anonymous tip, arrived to investigate and recovered the abandoned items, many of which belonged to missing persons reported in five states. Although the unusual discovery made headlines locally and nationally, the owners were never found. Their possessions remain unclaimed.

CREDITS

Stories in this collection originally appeared in the following publications:

"The Piazza de Chirico": *Art from Art: A Collection of Short Stories Inspired by Art* (Modernist Press, 2011)

"The Discovery of Dr. James Osborne Beckett": *The Last Word: A Collection of Fiction* (Unbound Press, 2012)

"The Presentation": *Have a NYC: New York Short Stories* (Three Rooms Press, 2012)

"The Well at Founders Grove": *Conjunctions* (online, 2009)

"The Abbreviated Life of Whitney Bascombe": *SPECS: Journal of Arts and Culture* (2009)

"Divination by Water": *PALABRA: A Magazine of Chicano & Latino Literary Art* (2008)

"Nuptial Superstitions of the West," originally published as "The Paranormal Guide to Wedding Etiquette": *A cappella Zoo* (2012)

"The Possession of Charles Ignatius De Leon": *Copper Nickel* (2012)

"The Devil and the Dairy Princess": *RE: TELLING: An Anthology of Borrowed Premises, Stolen Settings, Purloined Plots, and Appropriated Characters* (Ampersand Books, 2011)

"In the Empire of Cetaceans": *Arroyo Literary Review* (2011)

PEDRO PONCE teaches writing and literature at St. Lawrence University. His fiction has appeared in *Ploughshares, Alaska Quarterly Review, Gigantic, PANK, Copper Nickel,* and other journals. His work has also been anthologized in *The Best Small Fictions 2019, New Micro: Exceptionally Short Fiction,* and *Boundaries Without: The Calumet Editions 2017 Anthology of Speculative Fiction.* In 2012, he was awarded a National Endowment for the Arts fellowship for creative writing.

.

Lightning Source UK Ltd.
Milton Keynes UK
UKHW021536050921
389895UK00007B/38